Till Death Us Do Part
....and other short stories

I0596254

A Collection of Stories
from a life well-lived!

Written by
MAGGIE TAYLOR

This edition published in 2021 by Maggie Taylor
Edited by Tracey Regan
© Maggie Taylor 2021

ISBN : 978-0-6487192-9-8

Introduction

Some of these stories and poems came from my time at Midland T.A.F.E. doing a writing course. Like a lot of people, I have always wanted to write and like a lot of people I found any excuse not to sit down and do it! The writing course made me do my homework and after the course was finished, some of us formed a 'Writers Group.' We met monthly and had to produce a piece of new work for each meeting. It kept us all writing and I am very grateful for both the encouragement and criticism (both positive and negative!) I received. Over the years we have shrunk down to 3 members and I owe a big debt to Tracey and Karen for their continued support.

I hope you enjoy the result.

CONTENTS

Greed Is Not Always Good   1

Till Death Us Do Part   7

Kinky Hose - A Poem   21

The Front Room   23

The Neighbour   29

A Poem - In The Style of Mills & Boon   35

Puppy Love   41

The Deadly Sins - A Poem   47

The Attic   49

The Outpatients - A Poem   55

Revenge Is Sweet   59

Train Ride To Death   73

Puss In Boots - The Truth!   79

Vintage Days   83

The Retired Men - A Poem   87

What Comes Around   89

What's In It For Me?   97

Don't Get Mad - Get Even   107

The Power Of Words - A Poem   121

About The Author

Greed Isn't Always Good

Maria had an ironic smile on her lips as she listened to the Funeral Celebrant praising the 'Dear Departed'. She wondered what the Eulogy would have been like if the Celebrant had really known Des.

Her mind drifted back several years to when she had first met him. She had known Polly, his wife, for some time before and when they all met at an auction she was introduced to Des.

She hadn't liked him very much as he was quite arrogant and treated Polly with disdain, whilst drawing attention to how 'humble' he was – in fact she had christened him 'Uriah Heep' in her mind. Shortly afterwards he had left Polly to go and live with the first of many new ladies. Polly had been devastated but Maria thought it was the best thing that had happened to her in a long time.

Occasionally he would call into her home, which annoyed her greatly and he always seemed to leave with something she had discarded. They also met at the odd auction or sale yard as they were both interested in second hand items, but she noticed he rarely bid for anything and derided the prices that others paid. If he did bid it was usually for the 'cheap junk' items at the end of the auction.

One day he noticed Maria hadn't bid for anything either and when he queried it, she explained that she was planning to move and downsize so she was more interested in getting rid of stuff instead of acquiring more. She could have bitten out her tongue as soon as she had said it when she saw how his eyes lit up. That weekend Des came to her property and practically made an inventory. He wanted everything she wasn't taking with her, including the contents of several buildings that were going to be demolished. He offered to pay and Maria set a good price, which she thought would put him off, but to her surprise, he agreed to it. She squashed down her misgivings and rationalized the decision by telling herself that everything would be gone, she wouldn't have strangers all over the property and it was better than selling it in dribs and drabs at Garage Sales.

Time went by and Maria's plans to move advanced bit by bit, but Des hadn't moved anything or paid any money. She mentioned it to Polly one day and Polly laughed.

"Des has always been a 'gunna,'" she said. "He was always 'gunna' do it but never got round to it. Eventually I would get someone in to fix the washing machine or whatever and then he would get angry about how much it had cost, insisting he was going to fix it that very weekend, but of course he wouldn't have got round to it."

Eventually Maria got a date for demolition of the buildings and contacted Des, who finally turned up and started to move things. Then she realized he was simply moving them into another building that wasn't going to be demolished.

"Oh, no!" she said. If you want those things you have

to take them off the property or I will have a Garage Sale and get rid of them that way."

With a lot of muttering Des made a great show of turning up after work every day of the next week before demolition and taking stuff away in his car and an old trailer he had borrowed. Mostly Maria avoided him but one evening she was coming in just as he was leaving and stopped to ask how he much of the job he had completed. She was horrified to see several items in his car that were not included in the deal and had come from another building. When she confronted him he insisted she had told him he could have them. But Maria stood her ground and made him put them back.

The demolition was finally completed and the only item left for Des to take away was a small shed that had been a shade house. He had finally paid for the other items after many phone calls to remind him the money was 'still owing.' Several times he had taken her bank account details to 'pay direct' but each time he had 'lost' them or 'something came up' and he didn't have the money.

More time went by and there was no sign of movement in the shade house direction. Maria wasn't too bothered as she still hadn't put her property on the market but suddenly everything changed. She put an offer on a property and someone put one on hers. Again she contacted Des to tell him. In the intervening years Des had become quite obese and lazier than ever.

But he came in shortly afterwards and started to demolish the building. But several weeks went by and nothing more happened. Time was now running short and Maria gave him one last chance.

"You have two weeks Des," she said. "Then I am putting it in Quokka as I am moving at the end of the month."

Des protested that he had been very busy at work, he hadn't been well and it had been too hot and other excuses. Maria was obdurate.

"Two weeks Des," she said, and put down the phone.

That weekend he turned up with the latest lady in tow and started to pull down the building in earnest but again he was just moving it to another site, or rather the lady was whilst Des issued orders.

"No way Des," Maria said. "If you want it, take it away now or I can still put it in Quokka."

In spite of herself Maria felt a bit sorry for him It was quite a hot day and he was sweating profusely and a bit short of breath. But he had had the opportunity to let someone else have it after all. Des's problem was that he could never refuse a bargain and he was going to take the shed away if it killed him.

In the end, it did. He had just taken the final load when he had a massive stroke and died amid all the junk he had collected over the years and never done anything with.

Maria came back to the present as the Celebrant

was winding up the Eulogy. The slow ponderous music had started and the coffin was moving through the curtains to the flames beyond

"I hope they checked it before they screwed down the lid," she thought. "He could have half the chapel in there."

Till Death Do Us Part

As soon as Terri pulled the envelope out of her Post Office Box and saw her younger brother Sam's, barely literate writing, she knew what had happened. Sam had been dyslexic from childhood ever since he had his naturally-used left hand tied behind his back at Primary School, in order to make him use his right hand. He had also stuttered from the same time which had led to a lot of teasing. The same thing had happened to his Cousin, Geoffrey who was also a natural 'leftie,' so it took something of major importance for Sam to write anything – least of all a letter.

That was probably a misnomer because inside the envelope was a card and scrawled inside was:

Terri.

Sorry to tell you some bad news. Tom passed away on the 14th of May. We haven't got your phone number. Will you call me when you get this. Sam.

The news wasn't a shock to Terri. She had phoned her older brother for his birthday a few weeks previously and he hadn't sounded good then. He was 89 and had been in and out of hospital over the last few years. She had had a premonition that they wouldn't speak again and was glad she had made the effort to ring him.

However, the card made her very angry. Hadn't got her phone number! Admittedly she and Sam hadn't communicated much over the last twenty years, since her last return back to the UK in fact, but that wasn't unusual. She and Tom had always phoned each other for their respective birthdays and again at Christmas as they had a much closer relationship. He had always been her protective 'older brother' being nearly 10 years older, whereas there was only 4 years between her and Sam and they had always fought as kids; and that didn't improve much as adults.

But it wasn't Sam she was angry with. It was Tom's wife Carol. She knew Tom would have had her phone number written down and Carol would have known where to find it.

"That Bitch," she thought and remembered what had happened on her last visit to England.

She had been travelling with her friend Sally. They had picked up a Campervan after they arrived at Heathrow Airport and driven straight up to Tom's house in the Midlands, a journey of about three hours. They had stopped on the way to have lunch so they wouldn't need a meal as soon as they arrived.

Terri hadn't met her new Sister-in-Law before as she and Tom had only been married a few months. His previous wife, Marie, had died from breast cancer and although Terri only got back to the UK infrequently, she and Marie had always had a good relationship.

When they had arrived at Tom's house they had parked in the cul-de-sac where he lived. Tom and Carol were still eating their lunch in the kitchen and Terri thought the welcome was a bit frosty but maybe she had imagined it, especially after a 20-hour plane trip and no sleep for a lot longer, she was a bit fuzzy.

After the introductions Carol said,

"You can't sleep in the house. Tom snores and we sleep in separate rooms, so there's no room for you."

"No problem," replied Terri. "We can sleep in the Camper Van."

When Tom and Carol finished eating, they all retired to the sitting room for a cup of tea and to catch up. However, Carol dominated the conversation with minute details of her and Tom's wedding, complete with a large album of photos. After a couple of hours of this Terri tried to move the conversation along to other members of the family. She was particularly interested in Marie's niece Yvonne who had been like a daughter to her and Tom, so she was surprised when Tom said that they hadn't seen her for several months, since the wedding in fact.

As they seemed to be getting back to Carol's favourite topic again, Terri remembered the gifts she had brought with her, so she fetched them from the Camper Van. Tom was delighted with his book about the Australian outback as they had travelled around a lot on his only visit to the country, but Carol was less than impressed with her bag with an Aboriginal motif on it.

"I'm not into bags," she said and tossed it onto the window seat.

By now it was getting into the evening and even Carol seemed to have run out of wedding details.

"How about some food?" said Tom.

"I don't know anything about vegetarians," said Carol. "You said they would cook for themselves."

"That won't be a problem tomorrow," said Terri. "But we haven't got any food in yet."

"Well, what are we having Carol?" said Tom

"Chops and vegetables," she replied.

"We will be fine with just the vegetables," said Terri

After a tasteless meal of peas and potatoes jet lag was definitely catching up and Terri yawned widely.

"You must be tired," said Tom. "Would you like a bath or anything before you go to bed? I'll give you a key as well in case you want to come into the house to use the toilet in the night."

"That won't be necessary" said Carol. "They've got a toilet in the Camper Van and there isn't enough hot water for baths tonight."

Terri waited for some response from her brother but all he said was;

"Oh, all right then."

Sally had been very quiet all evening but as soon as they were in the Van she exploded.

"What is wrong with that woman? She obviously sees you as some kind of threat or something. What an absolute bitch."

Terri agreed, but said;

"Let's get some sleep and hopefully she will have settled down by morning."

That was a false hope as it turned out. Terri was the first up and dying to pee but not wanting to use the 'Porta Potti' which was really for emergencies only, made her way into the house only to be met by a furious faced Carol.

"I'm a straight talking person," she began, "and I have been very upset by your behaviour."

Terri's jaw dropped.

"What!" she said.

"You turned up yesterday without letting us know what time you would be arriving. No one in my family would ever do something like that. You interrupted our lunch with no apology and didn't bring any food with you."

Terri felt her temper rising rapidly but looking at her brother sitting miserably at the end of the table replied;

"I'm sorry if you were upset. But I rang you from Australia before we left and said we would be here around 2 pm depending on the traffic, which is what we did. Now if you will excuse me I need to use the bathroom."

When she got back to the kitchen Tom said hastily;

"What are your plans for today?"

"Well I would quite like to visit Mum and Dad's graves. I've never seen them and I'm not even sure where they are. I was hoping you might take us there."

"Tom has to paint the gutters today," said Carol.

Terri looked at her brother expecting him to say that the gutters could wait but instead he said;

"I'll draw you a mud map."

"Don't bother," said Terri. "We will be leaving this morning anyway and will find our own way there."

"You'll have some breakfast before you go though?" asked Tom

"No thanks," replied Terri. "I wouldn't want to put you out. We'll get something on the road."

Sally had packed up the Camper Van by the time Terri got back to it.

"Well was it better in the morning?" she asked.

"No worse, so I've said we are moving on today. Now, in fact."

"Thank God for that," said Sally, "or I might have punched her. There's nothing like the warm welcome that meets you from the rellies when you have come 12,000 miles to see them."

But that was the low point of their holiday and afterwards they had had a wonderful time travelling around England, Scotland and Wales.

In the intervening years she and Tom had exchanged letters as well as their infrequent phone calls. Hers had been many pages updating him about her family and their activities, but Tom's had been a page or two at most and usually about the weather or the cricket. Though he and Carol had moved to Spain at one point to be nearer Carol's son, that hadn't lasted long as Carol seemed to need constant medical appointments in the UK. Tom had mentioned in one letter how much money they had lost in the house transactions and they had eventually ended up back in the original town they had left.

Terri re-read the short note again and looked at her watch. It was too early to ring Sam yet as they were seven hours behind; Australian time. Then when she got home she couldn't find Sam's phone number either and had to go online to find it. Fortunately it wasn't a silent number and she eventually gave it a ring about 8 a.m. UK time.
Sam answered to phone and was full of apologies that he had lost her number.

"No problem Sam," said Terri, "I had to go on line to find yours."

"I'm not on line. I haven't gone in for all that technology."

"Well!" said Terri, "put me in the picture now. I last spoke to Tom on his birthday and I knew then he hadn't got much longer to go then. So what happened?"

"Apparently he had a fall in the bathroom and fell up against the door. Carol wasn't home but the District Nurse, who used to come in daily, found him. They had to break down the door to get him out and he had injured his shoulder in the fall so they took him to hospital but they only kept him in there for a few days before they wanted to send him home. That's when Carol rang us saying she couldn't cope and wanted us to have him here. She was all crocodile tears until we said 'no' as we were going on holiday the next day and he had a home to go to. However she manoeuvered it so he went into a Nursing Home and he died there a few days later."

"Your opinion of Carol seems a lot like mine," said Terri.

"Well we never liked her and she gradually cut Tom off from us. Every time we rang and suggested a catch up it was never convenient. In fact we hadn't seen them for about ten years."

"What," exclaimed Terri, "but you only live about half an hour away from each other. I thought it was a bit strange that whenever I asked Tom how you were he was a bit evasive and said you hadn't caught up recently. I thought you used to go motor racing and to the cricket together."

"That was BC – before Carol," laughed Sam.

Terri shook her head in disbelief.

"So what's happening now?" she asked. "Have you had the funeral yet?"

"No," replied Sam. "She is saying there is no money for a funeral. As soon as Tom died she moved out of the flat and took all the paperwork with her and went to stay at her nephews place. But the nephew seems to be a decent bloke and he told me there was 30,000 pounds in Toms bank account."

"That's what I would have expected," said Terri.

"Tom was always good with money Sam. There is no way he would have left her destitute. So what's behind this? Is she expecting that we will pay for the funeral?"

"That's what I am wondering, but it's not going to happen Terri. I do have a copy of the will though thanks to the nephew and there is a bequest for you and me in it."

"Well that is a surprise. I certainly didn't expect anything."

"No, neither did I. But don't go and book a cruise yet, we only get what's left after Carol dies and she'll make sure there's not much there."

"Meanwhile where is the body?" asked Terri. "He can't stay unburied forever."

"I'm not sure what's happening. I have to get back in touch with the nephew again. But I will get back to you as soon as I have any news. Now give me your number and I'll write it down so we don't lose it again."

After she had rung off Terri sat for a while trying to make sense of the situation. Then she went on line and did some research.

About a week later Sam rang again.

"Just updating you," he said. "She is still saying there is no money and unfortunately Tom made her Executor of the Will so she holds the purse strings."

"What about the flat, Sam. Is it being sold?"

"No, apparently they were renting it, they didn't own it. I don't know what to do about Tom's body Terri."

Terri sighed. Sam had always dodged responsibility and left any problems to Tom or her to solve. Nothing had changed.

"You know Sam," she said, 'there doesn't have to be a funeral. We can make arrangements for the body to be taken straight from the mortuary to the crematorium. I think if you want to be there you can but there isn't any sort of service."

"I didn't know you could do that," said Sam, "are you sure?"

"Well you can certainly do it here and I can go on line and check for the UK. I'm sure it's universal. I don't know how much it costs but I would be prepared to contribute to that if necessary. There is no way though I am paying for a funeral so that she can play the grieving widow."

"It seems a bit strange not to have a funeral though."

"Why, Sam? I'm not coming. I don't suppose Tom has many friends left alive to come and how many of our rellies are you in touch with these days? The ones in our generation are all long gone and the younger ones wouldn't even have met Tom – he wasn't very sociable. So that just leaves you and Carol. Tom wasn't religious in any shape or form so there's no church involved and he certainly isn't going to be worried one way or the other. You think about it Sam and I will do some more research and get back to you."

True to her word Terri phoned Sam again a few days later.

"How's it all going?" she asked.

"No change," replied Sam, "she is still sticking to the no money claim."

"OK," said Terri. "I have done some research and there are several companies that do the morgue to crematorium thing in your area. The cost is about a thousand pounds and that is door to door service literally. The only problem, apart from the money, is that Carol would have to agree to release the body as she is Next-of-Kin. How does that cost sit with you? Would you be prepared to pay half?"

"I suppose so, but it still sticks in my craw because I know the money is there," said Sam.

"I feel the same Sam, but Tom was a good brother and I hate to think of him left high and dry on a morgue slab somewhere. If you are prepared to go ahead with it, let the nephew know and we'll see what happens."

She gave him the details of the companies she had researched and left the next step to him.

But twenty four hours later the next phone call was from a furious Carol who launched into a diatribe of abuse as soon as Terri picked up her phone.

"How dare you deprive your brother of a proper funeral," she spat. "I can't believe you are such a mean, ungrateful sister. What will people think if he is just cremated, no one will be able to say goodbye properly. You are a hard hearted bitch. I am being insulted. He was my husband you know and I want the best for him."

Terri was tempted to hang up but she waited until Carol paused for breath and then said;

"There's nothing to stop you having a funeral Carol. You can have whatever you want, church service, new outfit, brass band – the choice is yours. All you have to do is pay for it."

"There's no money," screamed Carol. "Your brother has left me penniless. I am having to live with relatives because I can't afford to pay the rent on the flat."

This was too much for Terri.

"Just shut up with your lies about Tom," she said. 'Sam and I know that there was at least 30,000 pounds in his bank account when he died. If it's not there now it is because you have transferred it. If it is still there the Bank will release enough for a funeral and expenses to you as you are the Executor and his main beneficiary and his Next-of-Kin. You are the miserable, hard hearted bitch, denying Tom a funeral. Sam and I are not going to pay for it. You are bloody lucky that we have made the offer we have, but it's out of our love and respect for our brother that we are prepared to do that. Incidentally the offer is open for one week only from today then it will be withdrawn, so you had better make your mind up fast."

With that she hung up the phone. Immediately it rang again and it went through to answer phone and as soon as she heard Carol screaming at her she took it off the hook. Carol rang back several times over the next couple of days but it was only when Terri heard Sam's voice that she picked up the phone.

"I bet your ears are burning," he said with a chuckle. "I have had Carol on the phone so many times over the last couple of days and she is ropeable."

"Good. I hope you haven't changed your mind Sam. I told her she had one week from her phone call to me or I was going to pull the plug completely. Do you agree with that?"

"Absolutely and if she doesn't stop harassing me I will be withdrawing a lot sooner than that. It's like you said though, I contacted that firm you gave me details for and they can't do anything until Carol signs the consent form so the body can be released to them."

"Well then the ball is in her court Sam and I won't be losing any sleep over it. I think we are being more than fair and I am sure Tom would agree with it and I hope he haunts her. Keep me posted on any progress will you?"

"Sure, will do. Take care Sis."

But Sam's next phone call was unexpected news.

"You won't believe this," he said, "but Carol is dead. She had a massive heart attack apparently because she got so worked up that she wasn't going to get her own way. Her nephew has just rung me from the hospital and he is her Executor so he will be handling all the legal stuff. He is in favour of the no funeral thing and is going to do the same with her body and there is money to pay for both of them. I thought I might take Tom's ashes to scatter at the old family home in Clipsham. If you are thinking of coming over in the near future perhaps we could do it together. It would be good to catch up properly again.

The Kinky 'non-kink' Hose

It was in Bunnings I saw it, the Non Kink hose
at last I thought, I must have one of those.
It was a pretty, revolting cerulean blue
but if it stayed straight I'd forgive it its hue.
I lugged it to the checkout with a smile on my face
and couldn't wait to get home and put it through its pace.
It took a while to get it out of the pack
and to straighten it out was hard on the back.
But at last, there it was, the colour of sky
stretched out on the ground as straight as a die.
I plugged it into the tap and turned on the flow
it gushed out of the end as fast as it could go.
I dragged it around from one end to the other
and it followed along without any bother.
All went well for three months or so
then one day I noticed it was rather slow.
I followed it back and to my dismay
it had formed a little kink along the way.
I forgave it that one and straightened it out
but that hose was evil and knew what it was about.
From then on it was a battle between us two
it would kink at every chance it got, with nothing I could
do.
It would lie there like a malevolent snake
twisting itself into every shape it could make.

I cajoled, I threatened but nothing would help
it even tripped me up and made me yelp.
I gave it more time to settle itself down
then one day I saw red when it went to town.
So I got the tin snips out of the shed
and cut it in pieces until it was dead.
Then into a bin bag and off to the tip
over the side it went for its final trip.
So beware of false claims – too good to be true
or you could end up, very sorry for you!

The Front Room

The Front Room always had an air of mystery when I was a child, maybe because the door was always shut and no-one was allowed in there without permission. For a small child there was a battle between fear and curiosity.

It wasn't a very big room because this was a little 'two up' and 'two down' cottage. The ceiling was low and was held up by a black beam across the middle. There was a small window that opened (although it never did) straight onto the pavement of the village's main street. Its' curtains were always drawn though to discourage the curiosity of passers by.

Opposite the door was a fireplace with an elaborate mirror over the mantel, each side of which there was a black panel with a painting of flowers and a lot of gilt edging around the sides. On the right hand side of the fireplace there was a built in cupboard that was never used because it was so damp. It did prove very useful once though for growing 'mucor' a form of mould, on a piece of bread for a school science project.

The room had all the best furniture. In the middle was an extending oak dining table with six upright and uncomfortable chairs around it. Matching these chairs were two armchairs each side of the fireplace and a long low sofa under the window. They were upholstered in a blue/grey stripy and very prickly fabric

Along one wall was an oak sideboard, which was a veritable treasure trove. The cupboard held the 'best' crockery. It was white with a heavy gold border and included a very highly ornate teapot. I don't remember the teapot ever being used and the last time I saw it, the only thing it contained was my Mother's new and never worn, false teeth.

There were two drawers as well. The top held the 'best' cutlery, which always had to be cleaned before use as that was so seldom it was always tarnished. The bottom drawer was the most exciting though because in a pale blue 'handkerchief sachet' lived the family photos; old black and white ones of my Parents' youth, weddings, christenings, tinted studio portraits of the aunts, uncles and cousins, they were all there. Cameras were rare in those days and so were visits from the rellies so photos were very precious. They were the one thing I wanted from the family home and I was devastated to find that my Mother had burned them when she moved from the old cottage to a retirement complex at age seventy.

I think I realized then for the first time how she must have hated living in that pokey little cottage. She was far from her family and friends and in a little village where everybody was related and until you had lived there for about fifty years you were still seen as a foreigner. Mum also had no time for hypocrisy and said it as she found it. I thought of her the other day when I read an old Mongolian proverb:

"The man who speaks the truth needs to have one foot in the stirrup."

Mum didn't have any means of escape so she wasn't very popular, unless someone was dying or giving birth when she was always the one they called. So after the death of my Father, she could escape and she burnt the old life ready for the new.

But back to the front room. The floor was covered in a blue patterned lino with a 'rag' rug by the fireplace. These were usually made during the winter months from cut up old clothes. Initially there was a kerosene lamp in the centre of the table but this was replaced by a central light hanging from the ceiling when the village got electricity during the war, one of the few benefits from that inglorious event.

The remaining feature of the room was the cupboard under the stairs. It was just full of junk but I always found it a bit scary and had nightmares about being shut in it. Not that it was ever proposed, but I had a vivid imagination and read too much.

The only time the room got used was on Christmas Day. I'm not sure why because the chimney always smoked and the room stayed cold and damp until late in the evening no matter how early my Dad lit the fire. But ritual is ritual and Christmas Day was Front Room Day. For days prior to that there would have been a frenzy of cleaning and polishing, including the dreaded cutlery and for some reason the window that was rarely exposed, had to be cleaned too.

I have to admit it was quite impressive in the end. The best table cloth, starched and ironed, the gleaming cutlery, (with the odd blob of 'Silvo' where I hadn't rubbed hard enough), the posh crockery and of course the Christmas Dinner, eaten at 1pm on the dot. If it hadn't been for the cold, smoky atmosphere it would have been perfect.

But one day, it all changed. Up to that point I had shared the "Big Bedroom" with my two older brothers, but as puberty and High School approached, it was decided I needed a room of my own and the only one not being used was the Front Room. So the sofa and the sideboard were moved into the Living Room, the table stayed behind to be used as a desk for studying and the chairs were sold. My Mother must finally have accepted that they were never going to move into something better. My bed was carried down the twisty stairs and set up in the room. My Father built a wardrobe of sorts in front of the "Cupboard under the Stairs' so I could sleep at night and with a washstand and bowl I had literally a 'bedsit' – luxury after sharing with two smelly boys.

It also acquired an electric heater so no more smoky fires and I could do my homework in comfort, peace and quiet. I could also read at night when everybody else had gone upstairs to bed, because nobody could see my light was on.

The Living Room was much improved with the addition of the sideboard and sofa and so was Christmas

Day. In a warm, non smoky room, still with the best crockery and starched cloth, but the chairs were comfortable and the only drawback to this paradise was that the cutlery still had to be cleaned.

The Neighbour

"Oh God, what now?" sighed Alice, as she glanced out of the window and she saw her neighbour from across the road, striding up her drive. The door bell rang and she thought of ignoring it and pretending she wasn't in, but her car was in the drive and it was obvious she was home.

"Best get it over with," she said to her white Cairn Terrier, Jock, who headed for the kitchen.

She had barely got the door open when an ice cream container was thrust under her nose.

"He's done it again," said a very red faced Phyllis Curtis. "I am a very tolerant person, as you know Alice, but I cannot put up with this any more. It's the second time this week and I will have to complain to the Council if it happens again."

Alice made the pretence of looking into the container, but the smell had already told her what was there.

"I am sorry Phyllis," she said. "I did try to keep an eye on him this morning, but the phone rang as Tom was leaving for work and he must have slipped out of the gate whilst I was distracted."

"It's against Council Regulations to let dogs out in public without a lead as you well know," said Phyllis. "People who can't control their dogs shouldn't have them, I won't be warning you again." With that she turned and marched off down the drive, across the road and through her own gate.

As she closed her door Alice realised she was still clutching the container of dog poo and she started to laugh.

"If only she would ring me I would remove it," she said out loud.

She saw a small white face peering round the kitchen door.

"Oh Jock," she said. "Why do you do it? I think you like annoying her."

The little dog barked as if in agreement.

Later that evening, Alice told her husband Tom the story. As she expected, Tom's response was to laugh.

"Gives the old witch something to do," he said.

"It's not really a laughing matter, Tom. If she reports Jock, the Ranger could pick him up and take him to the Pound."

"Then we would just have to come and bail you out, wouldn't we, you old reprobate?" said Tom scratching Jock's head.

"But, Tom, she is on the Council. She knows all the rules and regulations and she has a lot of influence up there. Who knows what strings she might pull to get Jock put down."

"Don't worry Love," said Tom, "they have to keep them for at least 24 hours and I'm sure we would miss Jock before then."

"But if you could just be careful when you go to work and make sure he doesn't slip out of the gate, it would help."

"Well," said Tom, "if you could arrange it so I can back out my car without opening the gate, that might be possible. Besides I would have seen Jock going out the gate and I didn't, so I reckon he's found a hole somewhere. I'll have a good look tomorrow. Come on Alice you are letting old Phyllis get to you. It's hardly the crime of the century and a bit of doggy doo might give her lawn some character. Now I'm off to watch the telly, so let's not keep going on about it."

A couple of days later, Phyllis was on her way to a meeting. She had backed her car out of the garage and was walking back to close the garage doors, as her remote was being repaired. She turned to go back to her car and saw something white out of the corner of her eye. There in the middle of the manicured lawn was Jock, kicking grass and dirt over an obvious doggie dropping.

"You little wretch," shouted Phyllis launching herself towards him. "Just let me get my hands on you and ….."

Her shouts were interrupted by a screech of brakes and a loud thump. A car had come too fast round the corner and collided with Jock who had shot out in front of it. The car didn't stop, but roared off up the road.

Phyllis looked at the crumpled white heap on the side of the road. For a moment she felt triumphant, that he had got what he deserved, but she couldn't just leave him there. He was making the street look untidy. She would ring the Ranger to pick up the body and take it away, she decided as she walked over to the dog. But as she bent over him, Jock opened his eyes and gave a little whimper. He made a feeble attempt to stand up, but flopped down again and closed his eyes as if it had exhausted him.

Phyllis, for once in her well-ordered life, was in a dilemma. She had seen Alice leave earlier that morning and knew it was her day for volunteering at the Senior Citizens' Centre so she wouldn't be back before the afternoon. Jock was alive, so she couldn't leave him for the Ranger. The street was deserted as usual this time of day with most people at work or school. There was nothing for it. She would have to take him to the vet on her way to the meeting.

She unlocked the garage again and found a large plastic bag. She rolled Jock onto it and put him onto the floor of her car. She hoped he wouldn't make any mess. There was some blood on the side of his head, so she tucked the plastic securely round it and then drove off down the road.

The Vet was very sympathetic.

"I'm so sorry," she said, "you must be devastated."

"He's not my dog," snapped Phyllis. "He belongs to my neighbours."

"Well you have been a Good Samaritan then," said the Vet. "Have you let them know?"

"No," said Phyllis. "You can ring them when you have a clearer idea of the damage. Here's their number. I have a very important meeting to attend and all this has made me late."

Usually Phyllis was all attention in a Committee Meeting, most of which she chaired, but today her mind kept wandering to the picture of a small, white shape lying so silent and still by the side of the road. She found herself wondering if he was still alive. He hadn't looked too good when she had handed him to the Vet. She was puzzled by her feelings. Normally she couldn't stand dogs, nasty smelly creatures, or cats for that matter, who scratched the furniture, in fact animals in general disgusted her. If Jock died there would be no more nasty surprises for her to clear up, except Alice would probably soon get another dog. She had a soft heart for waifs and strays.

Finally, she could stand it no longer and as soon as the meeting ended, she rang the Vet surgery.

"He's holding his own," said the Nurse. "He's had a bump on the head and one of his legs is broken, but it looks like he'll survive. Tough little character isn't he?"

"Have you spoken to the owners yet?" she asked.

"Yes, said the Nurse. "I spoke to Mrs. Green. She was very upset of course and she's just left to go home."

Phyllis was also going home and as she drove into her driveway, she saw Tom getting out of his car in the driveway opposite, so he had obviously come home early.

She was about to go into her house when he called out to her.

"Phyllis, wait a minute."

She turned round to face him.

"I just wanted to say thank you for rescuing Jock and taking him to the vet. It was very kind of you, especially as he hasn't been your favourite animal lately. Look, Alice has just made some tea. Why don't you come over and have a cup whilst you tell us what happened?"

A Ballad
~ in the style of Mills and Boone

Like Mills and Boone the teacher said
so let's give it a whirl,
It needs a handsome hero
And, of course a gorgeous girl.

Now they have to have some names
I think I'll call him Jack,
It sounds strong and reliable
and goes with his six-pack.

Emma sounds OK for her
she'll have the right dimensions,
And lots of hair that's long and blond
maybe with extensions.

She'll have to have a rosebud mouth
blue eyes and long eye lashes,
Which she'll know how to flutter
when we get to the pashes.

Let's set it in a village
(I grew up in one of those),
He'll be a student on a farm
and she's the village rose.

Of course they have to fall in love
and it must be at first sight,
They'll spend days walking hand in hand
and kissing half the night.

But this is getting boring
it's needing something bad,
Like a snake in paradise
so, enter Charles the cad.

He is the Squires' only son
back home from foreign parts,
He's tall and dark and handsome
designed for breaking hearts.

Now Charles has got a roving eye
and also gift of gab,
He chats up pretty Emma
and he's very good – this lad.

Down our Emma's curvy spine
he quickly sends a shiver,
And it's hardly any time at all
before she's all aquiver.

Now it's choice of Jack or Charles
she's in a dilemma,
Which one does she love the most
and what is best for Emma?

Eventually she plumps for Charles
of course he has it all,
The car, the clothes, the money
and he's living at the Hall.

Poor Jack is devastated
How can he compete?
He only has a motorbike,
that Charles is hard to beat.

Jack begs and pleads with Emma
but she is obdurate,
She wants to be a model,
rich Charles shall be her mate.

So Jack departs the village
and goes far, far away,
Meanwhile Charles and Emma
are romping in the hay.

Then suddenly Charles just disappears,
overnight he's gone.
And he doesn't answer emails
or his mobile phone.

Even worse for Emma
she finds she's up the duff,
And with no-one to call Daddy
it's going to be tough.

The Squire doesn't want to know
what his Charles has done.
Emma's not the first young girl
to have fallen for his son.

Emma threatens D.N.A.
the Squire says 'go ahead.
You won't get a penny out of me,
you should have used your head.'

So Emma goes back home to Mum
getting bigger every day.
She sobs, she sighs, she fumes, she frets
but it doesn't go away.

Somehow there must be a twist
into this sad tale,
It needs a happy ending
can't leave her wan and pale.

Perhaps it's time to bring back Jack.
He's the hero after all,
And when things are getting desperate
he's the one to call.

The Farmer sends a letter
telling him what's new,
So Jack gets on his motorbike
and comes back right on cue.

He goes to see our Emma
and swears his love is strong.
He'll even keep the baby,
he just wants to right the wrong.

She protests that it's not right
for him to make amends,
Because the fault all lies with her
so perhaps they'll just be friends.

But Jack has seen the Parson
His motorbike he sells,
And everybody goes to church
to the sound of wedding bells.

Puppy Love

"He's so cute," said Liz Barlow as she cuddled the tiny puppy. Her husband Peter agreed.

"We've always wanted a long haired, miniature dachshund," he said. "Thanks for replying to our advert."

"No problem," replied the dog's owner, Jan Cunningham.

"How many were in the litter?" asked Liz.
Jan's expression changed suddenly as she frowned.

"There were only three," she said. "The other two didn't survive for very long after birth, though they seemed o.k. at first. Their mother Frieda, usually has five or six pups and she's always been such a good mother, but something seems to have gone wrong this time."

"Oh! What a shame," said Liz, "but this one is o.k. isn't he?"

"Yes. In fact I have never seen a puppy develop and grow so fast. He's only five weeks old but he's big enough for eight weeks already. I put it down to him being the only one and getting all his mother's milk – but Frieda has been very reluctant to feed him and it's been quite a battle. Maybe she is getting too old to breed any more. If this one had been a girl I would have kept her as a replacement."

"He is weaned though I hope," said Peter.

"Oh yes he's eating very well and has a monstrous appetite," replied Jan.

The Barlow's took the puppy back to their suburban home. They had fenced the back garden securely so he had plenty of space to run and play and still stay safe.

"We have to give him a name," said Liz. "How about something Germanic like Seigfreid?"

"He'll get called Siggy then. How about something shorter?"

They tried different names but nothing seemed quite right and the puppy slept on Liz's lap whilst they were talking.

"I know," said Peter jokingly. "How about Adolph?"

To their surprise the puppy jumped up and wagged his tail.

"Well he seems to like that," said Liz. "Hi Adolph!" The puppy made little yipping noises.

"Well that seems to be that," said Peter. "Adolph it is."

Adolph soon established a routine. The first night they had settled him in the laundry in his shiny new basket and a soft, cuddly blanket. But Adolph had voiced his displeasure in no uncertain way, whining and yipping for hours, until in desperation they had taken his basket into their bedroom. The next morning they had woken up to find him on their bed, under the doona, between them.

"How on earth did he get up here," said Liz. "I know it's a low bed but he has such short legs."

It was the same with food.

"Only feed him twice a day for the first six months

and then once a day will be quite enough," had been Jan's instructions.

But Adolph had his own ideas. He would sit by his dish and howl until something was put in it.

But he redeemed himself in other ways. They had installed a 'doggy door' so he could go into the garden for his toilet and he very quickly learned to use it. All their friends had warned them that it would be a nightmare for the first few weeks to train him, so they were surprised that after the first day there were no puddles or messes to clean up.

Liz was a Designer so she worked from home a lot. Adolph would sit by her side as she tapped on her computer but when he got bored he would demand attention and there would be no peace until she took him for a walk to the shops.

Two years passed and Adolph had grown into quite a large dog. People always commented on how gorgeous he was and he would look at them with his big, limpid brown eyes. Then one day a man asked Liz about his breed and when she replied that he was a long haired, miniature dachshund, the man laughed.

"There's nothing miniature about that dog," he said. "He's even big for a standard dachshund, I think he must be crossed with something else."

One day Liz had gone into the city and Adolph was at home alone. He was lying in the garden in his favourite sunny spot when there was a rustling noise nearby. He opened one eye and saw a white rabbit that belonged to the little girl next door sitting there eating some grass.

Like a flash Adolph grabbed it by the neck and shook it until it went limp, then he took it behind the garden shed, dug a big hole and buried it. When the neighbours asked Liz if she had seen it, Adolph was lying on a rug, fast asleep.
A few weeks later a friend of Liz called Gillian came round with her little white poodle.

"I wonder if you could do me a favour please Liz?" she asked. "I have to go to Sydney urgently and I can't get a flight back tonight. Could you look after Mimsie for me?"

"Not a problem," said Liz. "She will be company for Adolph as I have to be out all day today anyway."

"I've brought her food and basket," said Gillian. "Thanks Liz. I owe you."

"Before you go Gill," said Liz. "I have some news…. Peter and I are going to have a baby. I'm three months pregnant."

"Wow! What great news," said Gillian giving Liz a big hug.

"How exciting is that. Now you look after yourself."

Mimsie was not happy at being left behind and disappeared behind the sofa but Liz coaxed her out and she settled down a bit. When Liz left the house she said to Adolf,

"You'll have company today Adolph. Isn't that exciting. Now you two be good."

As soon as the car left the driveway Adolph pounced. He grabbed Mimsie by the neck and shook her until she went limp. Then he dragged her out through the dog door and down behind the shed, where he dug a hole and buried her.

When Liz got back and found the little poodle missing she was distraught. She drove around the neighbourhood and walked up and down the street asking at every house. When Peter got home he joined the search but there was no sign of Mimsie. They contacted the Police and the Pound in case she had been handed in, but Mimsie had disappeared from the face of the earth.

Gillian was heartbroken when they had to tell her the bad news. She said she didn't blame Liz but there was a cooling of the friendship between them.

Several months passed and Liz's pregnancy continued. They cleared out their spare room, painted it and bought baby furniture.

"I hope Adolph won't be jealous," said Liz.

"Of course not," said Peter. "He will still be one of the family and I am sure he will be thrilled to have a baby to look after."

Then one night Liz woke up in pain and Peter took her to the hospital. He was gone all night and when he came back the next morning he was very excited.

"We've got a little girl Adolph," he said and you will have to help look after her."

Adolph looked at Peter with his big limpid eyes and went and lay down on his rug.

Several days later Liz came home with the baby.

"Look Adolph," she said. "This is Amanda. Isn't she beautiful?"

Amanda opened her eyes and then her mouth and cried and cried. The house was soon in turmoil. There were day feeds and night feeds and washing and visitors. Adolph still got fed but there was no time for walks as Liz was always busy and the visitors only had eyes for the baby. No-one took much notice of Adolph except Liz's mother.

"You'll have to watch that dog Liz," she said. "They can get very jealous you know and you have spoilt him such a lot."

"Adolph's fine Mum! He loves Amanda. He spends hours just watching her."

Peter went back to work after a couple of weeks and Liz was on her own.

One day she had been shopping and when she got home Amanda was asleep in her capsule, so she brought her into the house first and put her on the floor by the open French window as it was a warm day. Then she went back to the car to get the shopping. Her neighbour called to her and the two women chatted over the fence for a few minutes.

When she came in with the shopping the capsule was empty and as she looked out of the window she saw Adolph coming up the garden from the direction of the shed.

The Deadly Sins

The Deadly Sins – I've done them all
sometimes big and sometimes small.

Let's start with Lust – it gets bad press
but it makes life fun and gives it zest.

Greed is good the city says
but eat too much and see who pays.

Gluttony makes greed seem pale
ask King John who drowned in ale.

To Sloth I think we all relate
slumped by the telly from morn till late.

Who do you Envy, what have they got
that you can't afford – let's hope they rot.

Hm! That begins to sound like Wrath
a biblical word without much froth.

But Pride won't let us own our sins
we pretend we don't care who wins.

In life's race to reach the top
but without these seven we'd be a flop.

The Attic

I always liked the attic as a child so I often went up there to play, sometimes with a sibling but mostly on my own. I was the youngest of seven living children and had been born very late in my parent's lives. The nearest sibling to me in age was 12 years older than me so I was practically an only child from the companionship point of view. The attic seemed a safe, warm and friendly place then but little did I know how it would change and affect my life.

I had my first attack of the 'falling sickness' when I was eight years old. Suddenly I was lying on the ground twitching and shaking. I lost control of my bladder and to my shame, wet my knickers. Then they came more and more frequently. The Doctors bled me and gave me Mercury but nothing helped. After several humiliating experiences in public, both to me, and my parents, I was put in the attic for my own safety and I suspect their pride.

I had my books and could draw and write. I was well fed and cared for but most of the time I was on my own. Most of my siblings had left home and the remaining ones soon got tired of me or had other, more important, things to do in their lives. Eventually I was left with my elderly parents and as the stairs to the Attic were steep and rickety they made their visits as infrequent as possible.

Then there came a day when they didn't come at all. I would learn later that they had succumbed to a vicious form of influenza that was spreading rapidly through the countryside and were both dead.

The Attic door was bolted on the outside and there were bars on the window so there was no escape for me. I couldn't attract attention from anyone because nobody came to the farm very often. It was very isolated and one of the neighboring farmers leased the land. There were no animals any more apart from a few chooks and an old horse. My father, now in his eighties, used him to pull a small cart into the nearest town, a two hour journey away, about once a month to pick up the mail and supplies.

Two of my brothers didn't come back from the Great War, and the other had emigrated to Canada before it started, as he realized the farm wasn't big enough to feed three families. One of my sisters had died in childbirth. One was a Missionary in Africa and the other lived on the other side of the country with her husband and brood of children. So nobody realized what had happened until it was too late for me. Inevitably I starved to death, although I did once eat a mouse I caught, fur and all. My ghost has haunted this house ever since. Angry and resentful about my wasted life I could not move away until someone had paid, and pay they did.

Eventually the bodies were found, including my emaciated one, but after a bit of a furore the story was forgotten. The epidemic had been devastating and there were many horrifying stories and most people chose to believe that I had died from it too. Eventually the farm was sold and new people came to live in the house.

The first couple were middle aged and had no children. The man was a mean and nasty character who had bought the farm because it was so cheap. It was a time of the Depression when many people were walking off their farms and they could be picked up for a pittance. His wife was a shriveled up husk of a woman. She was totally browbeaten and lived in fear of her husband especially when he had been drinking. One night he had beaten her pretty badly and was slumped across the kitchen table in a drunken stupor, so I got into her head and said:

"Kill him now. You will never get this chance again. Hit him on his head with the empty bottle. Go on do it."

Because she was so used to doing what she was told, she obeyed me and brought the bottle crashing down on his head again and again. Then realizing what she had done, she rushed out of the house and threw herself down the well.

The farm stayed empty a long time after that as people began to think it was a place of ill omen. I helped that by appearing at the attic window as a light at night or as a face during the day if any one came near. Being a ghost has a lot of advantages, as you are not restricted by the limitations of the flesh.

But times changed and farms became prosperous again after the Second World War so eventually a neighboring farmer bought the land to add to his. New people moved into the house. They were a Polish couple, refugees from the turmoil in Europe and had two boys. One was about twelve and his young brother was about four. Apart from making the place very cold if they came near the attic I left them alone until the little boy drowned in the Dam.

This was nothing to do with me I assure you, but a lot to do with his older brother who held him under the water. Then he claimed he had got so wet trying to pull his little brother out.

The ghost of the little boy came to me and together we planned his revenge. The older boy was a bully who terrorized smaller children and was very cruel to the farm animals. One day, when he was walking by the Dam, the ghost of the little boy appeared pointing an accusatory finger at him. The bully was petrified and rushed home a blubbering mess. After that it was easy. The hauntings became more and more frequent both day and night until the older brother couldn't stand it any longer and hung himself from a beam in the barn.

The parents moved away soon after that and the ghost of the little boy went with them.

Then there was talk of demolishing the old house but accommodation was at a premium and several families came and went for the next few years. Mostly they went because I made sure the place was always freezing. No matter how much wood they piled onto the stove it made no difference. They couldn't get warm in their beds, not even in

Summer. The owner tried insulating the roof but nothing helped, freezing it remained.

But one day a young woman and her small daughter moved in. The Mother was a writer who wanted solitude and the little girl was quite frail so she was schooled at home.

They cleaned up the old place, putting in soft rugs and bright cushions and curtains. The old stove was polished and had a warm fire most of the time. There was a lot of love and laughter and they had many friends to stay. I retreated to the attic but one day the little girl made her way up the stairs. I instantly put out the freeze but she ignored it and came on into the attic, even looking out of the window. Later I heard her talking to her Mother downstairs.

"Mum did you know there was an attic? I love it. Can I have it for a playroom please? Do you know why there are bars on the windows? Can they come off please?"

Her mother laughed and said, "Let's go up and have a look shall we?"

Very soon the attic was transformed into a cosy playroom and the little girl spent most of her time up there. I watched her play as she reminded me of my childhood when life had been happy.

But one day a terrible thing happened. She suddenly fell to the floor with the 'falling sickness.' I watched in horror as she twitched and shook uncontrollably, frothing at the mouth and turning a horrible blue colour. Her Mother must have heard the crash as she hit the floor because she flew up the stairs and held the little girl until she recovered. I thought that she would put her daughter in the attic just like me, but she helped her up to her feet after a while and said,

"Darling, I am so sorry. We will have to increase your medication again. I have been a bit slack because you have been so well since we got here. I didn't think about how much bigger you have grown."

She then helped the little girl down the stairs. I was left in the attic happy that things had changed so much in a hundred years, so no little girls would need to be shut in attics ever again. Finally I was released from my anger and resentment and although I could have moved on, I chose to stay at the farmhouse and watch the child who might have been me all over again, grow up in freedom.

A Ballad
~The Outpatients Clinic

One fifteen our appointment said
so why are so many others there.
Within ten minutes the place is full
and it's difficult to find a chair.

All nationalities are represented.
United like sheep we sit and stare
at the ads on Channel 9
before 'Days of our Lives' is featured there.

One hour has passed and still we wait.
Occasionally a name gets called.
Some lucky person rises and goes
into a cubicle, but our life has stalled.

Around us all is bustle.
Nurses rush up and down with notes
and Doctors emerge from cubicles
with stethoscopes and long white coats.

It's interesting watching other people.
Some fidget, some read and some talk
but most just sit in silent resignation
or in desperation go for a walk.

We've been here for nearly two hours.
We've watched most of 'Days of our Lives'
including a very steamy sex scene
which passed before our eyes.

But, at last, our name is called
and we sigh with relief as we rise
only to come back five minutes later
to wait thirty more with drops in our eyes.

The hands on the clock pass slowly
more people keep coming in.
Some standing along the sides now
and their patience is wearing thin.

There have been a few diversions
someone lost a vital key
and an old bloke in a wheel chair
announces he needs to pee.

Thirty minutes must be up
perhaps they've forgotten we're here.
There were fifteen lots of notes in the pile
that our Doctor still has to clear.

But no, someone is waving at us
from the end of the corridor.
So back to the cubicle for five more minutes
before we're ushered out of the door.

Three and a half hours since we arrived
and ten minutes of actual care.
But we aren't stopping to complain
as we just want to get out of there.

That we have to come back again next week,
is the only fly in the ointment.
We have to see someone else it seems
so we've got another appointment.

Revenge Is Sweet

He felt very conspicuous standing by the University gates in his business suit and tie as crowds of students poured out in every type of dress but his – jeans, sweat shirts, frills, Indian, Malaysian and it seemed the more garish and outlandish the more popular it was. Why on earth had Catherine asked him to meet her here and not in the city. Since their marriage broke up a year ago she had changed. Before he would have fixed the meeting place and she would have complied, no matter how inconvenient to her. He wasn't sure he liked the change but he needed her on side at the moment. If they could get the divorce over amicably that would be one pressure less. Goodness knows he had enough worries on the business side with the slump in mining making Geological Consultants as necessary as a hole in the head to most Mining Companies.

His musings were interrupted by a slight scuffle in the gateway as a vivacious, dark haired women with a group of younger students, had turned to say something over her shoulder and slipped on the worn steps. One of the young men had grabbed her arm to prevent her falling.

"Thanks Mike" she said, giving him a warm smile.

"Think nothing of it Kate," he said with a mock bow. "We have to look after you elderly students. Can't have spontaneous fractures all over the Campus you know, bad for the image."

The woman laughed and seemed about to retort when she caught sight of Charles.

"Oh! Hi Charles," she said, moving away from the group towards him.

They continued on with curious glances in his direction.

"Don't forget the Prof prompt at two Kate," said one of them as they moved on down the road.

"I won't," she replied and turned back to Charles. "How are you?" she asked looking at him searchingly. "You look tired."

"Hello Catherine, I didn't recognise you for a moment. You look different, your hair is much longer and you've got thinner."

His voice trailed off as the truth hit him, his wife looked much younger, without makeup, but sparkling with vivacity and yes, he had to admit, very attractive in her tight jeans and sweater.

"Why did they call you Kate?" he asked abruptly.

"Oh well, I thought a new life and a new image you know. Goodbye Catherine, middle-aged respectable wife and mother and hello Kate, fancy free with only myself to please. It's marvellous Charles I feel a different person. You should try it sometime. Now to be practical, I have to be back for a lecture at 2pm, that's why I suggested you meet me here. There's a little Italian Restaurant around the corner which is fairly quiet this time of day and you can have anything from a cup of coffee to a full meal, so if that will suit you I suggest we go and find it."

He found himself walking briskly by her side. The pace didn't allow for conversation and they quickly reached the restaurant.

A rotund Italian man welcomed them with a broad smile.

"Gooday, Kate," he said. "You like to sit by the window today?"

"No thanks Luigi," she replied. "We have business to discuss so a quiet table at the back where we won't be interrupted please."

"Of course, you come this way please," and he led them to a corner table at the end of the small room thrusting a menu towards them as they sat down.

"Just lasagne and a coffee for me please Luigi," said Kate. "I can recommend it Charles unless there's something else you would prefer?"

"No, I'll have the same thanks," said Charles, marvelling silently at the poise with which the whole manoeuvre had been completed.

Kate took off her dark glasses and placed them on the table. Without them she didn't look quite so young as there were fine lines around her eyes and the frown line between her eyebrows seemed a bit deeper than he remembered.

"Now Charles," she said. "Why did you want to see me so urgently?"

This wasn't quite the way he had planned it. A softening up with some fine wine in a secluded restaurant and the right ambience would have helped with the old Catherine, but this stranger sitting opposite him wasn't her. He cleared his throat and said, hesitatingly;

"Well, we've been separated over a year now and legally we can apply for a divorce, if that's what you want of course," he added hastily.

"Is that what you want Charles?" she said quietly keeping her eyes fixed on his face. "Do you and Estelle want to get married?"

They were interrupted momentarily by a beaming Luigi with the lasagne and two glasses of wine.

"The vino issa on the house, and the coffee she come later, o.k?" he said, and hurried away to serve other customers.

Charles pushed a fork full of food into his mouth and chewed determinably before replying, his thoughts busy. Did he and Estelle want to get married? Estelle certainly did and it was she who had urged him to see Catherine and get it settled as soon as the time limit was up. After all they had been living together for a year and sleeping together before that for quite some time before Catherine found out.

It had been so easy somehow. When he had taken her husband, Mark, on as a partner in his thriving consultancy business, he had no way of knowing that six months later he would be killed in a light plane crash whilst going out to one of the outback mining sites.

Estelle was inconsolable at first. She and Mark had come out from England for the job and she had no relatives and not many friends apart from him and Catherine, in Australia. Catherine had been wonderful; inviting Estelle to stay with them in Mandy's bedroom. Mandy was doing what every eighteen year old seemed to be doing nowadays and having a gap year abroad.

They had thought that Estelle would go back to England as soon as the inquest was over but somehow she had stayed on. It was Catherine who had pointed out that Estelle was a Geologist too and could take over Mark's job for a while, it might lift her out of the depression that seemed to have settled over her like a cloud.

It had worked too. Estelle had in fact turned out to be better than Mark. She was twenty nine, very smart and attractive and a novelty to Australian mining companies and she had certainly charmed several big contracts their way. In fact they had become so busy that they often had to work late together at the office and it became convenient to have a meal at the flat Estelle had moved into close by.

Quite when the relationship had changed he wasn't sure, but, gradually he had stayed later and later at the flat and they had become more attracted to each other. All this time Catherine had said nothing. She frequently invited Estelle in for a meal and was as friendly as ever to her.

Adrian, their son, was still at school at this stage and

Catherine, as she always had, was involved in his school activities and the numerous Charities she worked for. She frequently attended meetings and it was whilst she was away at a weekend Conference that he and Estelle had become lovers. Adrian was away at a school camp that same weekend and there was no reason to go home. They were working against a deadline on a new contract and after they had had a late meal at the flat, Estelle had said;

"Why don't you stay the night Charles?"

It was an innocent enough suggestion as there were two bedrooms in the flat, but they both knew that wasn't what she meant and once they had slept together the whole thing progressed rapidly.

Then came the contract in Indonesia.

"I think I ought to take Estelle with me Catherine," he had said. "It will be good experience for her in a foreign country and then she will able to go on her own another time."

Catherine's reply had been evasive but she had driven them to the airport and waved them off.

The two weeks they were away had been like a honeymoon with no one to query their comings and goings and Charles knew at the end of it that they had to make a decision. Catherine had to be told the truth. At first Estelle demurred as she didn't want to be 'the other woman' and Catherine was her friend, but eventually she agreed that it wasn't fair to go on deceiving her.

However no Catherine met them at the airport and, on reaching his house, Charles had found a note saying she had taken Adrian away for a few days after his final exams and added at the bottom was, 'you might want to move your things out whilst we are away – it will be less painful for us all that way.'

Bemused by her perspicacity Charles had nevertheless taken his belongings and moved in with Estelle. Later he and Catherine had met to discuss the situation and she had surprised him again by saying;

"I am going back to University next year and being so far out of town will be a problem. Adrian is going up North for a year to work on a Cattle Station and Mandy will be starting her Nursing training so as none of us need this house any longer let's sell it and divide the proceeds. I will get a flat near Uni and the children can stay when they want to. You and Estelle will doubtless make your own arrangements."

"I can make you an allowance," said Charles.

"No thanks," came the quick reply. "I am quite capable of managing. I can get a grant and I will invest the money from the house."

"What about Plato and Claudia" queried Charles. "I can't see a Labrador in a flat."

"Not a problem, that is all sorted. Jan and Peter will take him. He's always liked them and their old dog died recently as it happens. Claudia will come with me. Siamese don't mind flats and she hardly goes outside anyway, but I will try to get something with a courtyard."

"I don't know what to say Catherine, you are so calm and organised."

"Well I have had time to get used to the idea Charles. I am not blind or stupid you know. I can't say I am happy at the moment, but they say time heals everything so I'll busy myself whilst I am waiting."

Things had happened quickly after that. The property was a very attractive one in a natural bush setting and it sold within six weeks. Catherine took what furniture she wanted for her flat but not very much because she said it was all too dark and heavy for a small place. Most of the rest was sold with the house to a Scottish Doctor and family who had just emigrated with the bare necessities and were overjoyed to get a readymade home.

Mandy was upset by the separation at first but within a few weeks of starting her Nursing Course seemed to have adjusted and became quite friendly with Estelle. Adrian appeared quite philosophical about the situation but was noticeably cool towards his father and avoided Estelle as much as possible.

Charles swallowed the lasagne and then said;

"Yes, Catherine, Estelle and I want to get married."

"Well I have no problem with it Charles though I haven't investigated the procedure as I have been too busy to think about it. Studying takes up a lot of time and it took a while for my brain to get back into gear."

"What exactly are you studying Catherine?"

"Archaeology and Ancient History – a double major as I couldn't decide between them and they go well together."

"Wow! I didn't know you were interested in in either of them."

"I am not surprised," retorted Kate. "You were never interested in anything I did Charles."

"Well it seemed to be all about the children Catherine and I left all that side to you as I was away so much earning our living. It wasn't all fun and games you know."

"Yes I noticed. Now back to the divorce. Can you find out what we have to do? I have exams coming up and will be flat out for a few weeks. Then I am going on a 'dig' over Christmas and New Year in Ethiopia with my Professor and a group of other students so I will be away until February."

"What about Christmas?" asked Charles. "What will Adrian and Mandy do?"

"No idea but I am sure they will survive. They are 19 and 21 now you know. They can always come to you and Estelle."

"No, we are going to the Gold Coast so we won't be available."

Luigi came to the table with two cups of coffee and picked up their plates.

"All ok?" he asked brightly.

"Lovely, as always," said Kate.

They chatted about general things as they drank their coffee and then Kate looked at her watch.

"Oh God!" she said. "I am going to be late."

She put some money on the table.

"Here's my share Charles. Could you pay the bill please. Nice to see you and let me know what I have to sign. Love to Estelle," and she rushed out of the café before Charles could reply.

Six months passed and finally the divorce papers were ready but Charles hadn't contacted Catherine again and he noticed Estelle hadn't mentioned marriage recently either. The mining slump was over and they had been very busy, so much so that they had taken on Paul, another Geologist. He was in his late twenties and very bright, reminding Charles of himself twenty years earlier. He and Estelle got on well and he frequently came round for dinner so they could continue their business discussions over the meal.

It was at one of these evenings that Estelle reminded them that there was an important dinner coming up which all the influential people in the mining world usually attended and she had bought tickets for all three of them.

Charles was a bit surprised and a bit disappointed as he liked attending those occasions with his attractive partner on his arm. However, it would seem churlish if he said that Paul couldn't go with them, but he did try to find an excuse to send him out of town that night. However, when the evening duly arrived, all three of them set out with Paul looking particularly handsome in his 'tux'.

As they were walking into the venue, Charles was hailed by an old acquaintance and paused to greet him. When he turned round Estelle and Paul had continued on into the building. He hurried to catch up with them and almost bumped into Kate.

"What are you doing here?" he asked abruptly.

"I am partnering my Professor, Charles. May I introduce Donald Sullivan. Don, this is my ex-husband Charles."

A tall man with a greying beard and very blue eyes held out his hand.

"Pleased to meet you Charles," he said "Kate has talked about you and I believe you are a Geophysicist with your own business. Well done you, it's not easy in mining is it?"

"No it isn't Don. But what brings you here. Archaeology and mining don't seem to go together."

"Actually they do Charles. We have to keep abreast of possible mining leases around our 'digs' especially in third world countries. A lot of those governments aren't averse to selling off land without a lot of consultation."

"Don is one of the speakers tonight Charles," said Kate, "so you will hear all about it. Now we had better go in."

As they walked up the steps she continued;

"Where's Estelle tonight? Have you set a date for the

wedding yet?"

"She's gone ahead," replied Charles, ignoring the last question. He kept looking at Kate. She was blooming. Her long dark hair was held back with a diamante clip and her simple black dress showed off her slim figure to perfection. He was aware that several men gave her a second glance but she was holding Don's arm, not his.

Finally they were inside the Ballroom where the dinner was being held and he looked around for Estelle. She was on the opposite side of the room, holding a drink and chatting animatedly to Paul. They seemed oblivious to everybody around them and were making a lot of eye contact.

Charles felt his stomach churn. Maybe this was why Estelle hadn't been mentioning marriage lately. He was aware that Kate was giving him a sympathetic look.

"Is everything alright with you and Estelle?" she asked.

"Of course," he snapped. "Why wouldn't it be?"

"Well she does seem very interested in that handsome young man she is with."

"He works with us, he is a Geologist and his name is Paul, that's all there is to it." But he knew instinctively that it wasn't. He changed the subject.

"What about you and the Professor then?" he asked. "What's the story there?"

"We are getting married as soon as the divorce goes

through, so let me have those papers soon Charles. We'd like to have a honeymoon in Jordan. There's a 'dig' there next year so it would all fit in wonderfully. I don't think I have ever been so happy before and I do hope you will come to the wedding."

Train Ride To Death

He picked her out as soon as she walked down the platform of the city railway station. She was in her sixties judging by her white hair but smartly dressed in what looked to be expensive clothes. She was wearing sunglasses and carrying a large tote bag, both 'designer' he thought.

She was slim, average in height and in spite of a slight limp she carried herself well. He followed her into a carriage of the waiting train and sat down opposite to her. It was 'senior's card time' after 9.30 a.m.so the train wasn't very full and most of the other passengers were elderly too.

He pretended to be looking at the screen of his mobile phone but in reality he was watching her. She was wearing an expensive looking gold watch and had several gold chains around her neck. Her wedding ring and diamond engagement ring on her left hand were matched by two other large rings on her right hand.

Then an elderly man sat down beside her and they started to talk to each other. He had never understood why older people seemed to need to talk to each other and decided it was a generational thing. They were discussing the article on the front page of the newspaper the man was carrying.

"He seems very hard to catch," said the woman.

"Well the police are underfunded and undermanned," replied the man, "so it's not surprising that these people get away with so much these days."

"But he always strikes in broad daylight and no-one ever seems to see him. It's only when they find the body that they know a crime has been committed."

"That's because life is more dangerous these days than when I was young," replied the man. "I fought in two world wars and I didn't feel as insecure then as I do now. I hesitate to go out of my house sometimes."

"Oh dear, that's a shame," said the woman shaking her head. "We should be able to walk down the street safely. I can remember when we didn't even lock our doors or our cars at night and that's not so long ago."

The train slowed down for the next station and the man stood up.

"Nice talking to you," he said, "but this is my stop so I'll say goodbye.

"Goodbye!" said the woman. "Stay safe."

He was pleased that the man had got off- altogether too chummy he thought. It could have been a problem. But now the woman was collecting her things and standing up ready to get off at the next station. He followed her off the train but kept well back and blended in with the other passengers on the platform.

It was quite an 'upmarket' area and he hoped she didn't have someone meeting her, but she kept walking out of the station and along a nearby street. For her age she was a surprisingly fast walker. They were approaching a café strip and he thought she was going to stop but she had just slowed down to look in a shop window before she turned left into a quiet residential street.

About halfway down she turned into the driveway of a well maintained, federation style house. Although quite old these houses had soared in value over the recent years and the suburb was one of old money and conservative traditions, mostly populated by the elderly who had bought their houses many years before. Although most of the houses had been renovated and updated they had kept their original facades.

It was getting better and better as far as he was concerned because these houses all had a laneway behind them. It was designed initially for the 'night soil' cart but now it provided access to their back gardens.

He waited until she had unlocked the front door and gone inside, then he walked past and kept going until he reached the next cross street where he turned left. Sure enough there was a laneway and he sauntered along it until he was behind the woman's house. He knew it was the right house because he had studied the colour and shape of the roof but it had a high wall and a secured gate opening on to the laneway. Fortunately the house next door only had a wire mesh fence and an easily opened gate. He paused a while but no-one stirred and no dogs barked so he went into that garden. The dividing fence was an asbestos one and the supporting wooden framework was on his side so it was easy to climb up and look over it.

There were plenty of mature shrubs and trees on the other side to give him cover so he rapidly climbed over the fence and dropped down into her garden.

Again he waited but there was no sign of life so using the cover of the shrubs he made his way slowly along the fence towards the house. The garden was terraced and the area closest to the house was an open lawned area with some garden chairs and a table on it. But again he traversed it quickly and no-one seemed to have seen him.

Now he was up close to the house and he saw a glass French window which allowed access to the garden. He edged along towards it and to his surprise it wasn't locked. Cautiously he peered into the room. It was furnished as a dining room with a long table and eight chairs and a sideboard along the wall. No one was visible so hardly believing his luck he went inside.

At one end of the room was a kitchen and the other end opened out into a large sitting room. Both rooms were deserted so he walked into a passageway which opened off the dining room. There were several doors each side of it, presumably bedrooms and bathrooms he thought. Still moving silently he crept along it and opened doors slightly as he passed but there was no sight of the elderly woman.

Until he came to the end of the passage and there was one door left. It was half open and there she was, lying on a bed with her eyes closed. Her shoes lay on the floor where she had kicked them off.

He could almost feel his hands around her throat and see her death struggles as she fought for breath. He moved towards the bed and reached over to make it reality, when she suddenly shot upright and grabbed him around his neck in a strong grip and twisted his body down onto the side of the bed. At the same time footsteps raced down the hall and the elderly man rushed into the room, pinioned his arms behind him and slapped on handcuffs.

"Got you, you bastard," said the elderly woman who was looking a lot less elderly now her wig had fallen off in the struggle exposing blond hair. The elderly man had also undergone a surprising rejuvenation as he stood over the man on the floor.

"WPC Helen Drummond," said the woman, "and I am arresting you for attempted murder and I am sure we will find your DNA matches that found at the site of four other murders of elderly women who have been murdered and robbed in the last six months.

"Detective Sergeant Adrian Murray," said the 'elderly' man. "You should have varied your M.O. Charlie. It was only a matter of time before we made the connection that all your victims had been riding on a train shortly before they were killed in their houses, though it was interesting watching you creep up to the house."

"But you got off the train," stuttered, Charlie.

"No, that was just an illusion Charlie. I got back on again in another carriage, so I was following you, following her - piece of cake really. Now on your feet, there's a Police car waiting in the drive to take you to the next phase of your life – incarceration. Let's go and well done Helen! You'll make a very spunky old lady when you get there."

Puss In Boots
~ the truth !!

This is the tale of Puss in Boots
but not the one you've heard.
That's a load of rubbish
so don't believe a word.

Puss was just a simple cat
who had no fancy gear
just a common tatty moggy
the other cats would jeer.

Until, one day, he chased a rat
across a busy road
and scared some fancy horses
with a very special load.

T'was the King and Princess Glamorous
out in their carriage sound
but when it all got overturned
they landed on the ground.

Now Puss's owner, Jack the Lad
had just done his First Aid
and he rushed out from his cottage
to save the fair young maid.

He quickly gave her mouth to mouth
and pressed her curvy chest
until she spluttered 'I'm O.K.
but what about the rest.'

Under the carriage wheels lay
a body with arms attached
and when he found two legs as well
all the pieces matched.

But he couldn't find the head at all
and he knew the King was dead
so when he spied a golden crown
he put it on his head.

Just to get it out the way
whilst he did his best
with haemorrhages and broken bones
for the Footman and the rest.

Then a group of peasants came
from a nearby field
when they saw the crown upon Jack's head
'Your Majesty' they squealed.

The Princess by now was sitting up
and quickly got the gist
but the peasants all had pitch forks
so she didn't dare resist.

'You are my hero Jack' she said
'and since poor Daddy's gone
I think you'd better marry me
and we will share the throne.'

But Jack began to stammer
'I can't marry you,' he said.
'I'm the only Gay in the village
and I couldn't share your bed.'

Poor Princess Glam was quite upset
but she tried to keep her cool
'then give me back the crown,' she said,
'for I will have to rule.'

Jack took the crown from off his head
and handed it to her.
'I don't want to be King,' he said,
'my life I much prefer.'

'Jack you're such an honest man,'
said the Princess overawed
'but there has to be some recompense
so you choose your reward.'

Jack said, 'I'd like the Footman
so if you could leave him here
he could be my boyfriend
and my future would be clear.'

The Princess said 'O.K. with me
if it's alright with Jim.'
'Ooh, yes please,' said the Footman
'cos I quite fancy him.'

So King and carriage were towed away
and the Princess went back home
to her castle on the hill
with the shiny, golden dome.

Jack went back to his cottage
with the Footman and his cat.
They lived happy ever after
thanks to Puss Cat and a rat.

Vintage Days

If you were a car over sixty years old you'd be called 'vintage'. You would be fussed over, regularly checked-up on, polished, handled with kid gloves – treated like Royalty in fact. So how much more important than a car are you? Why do we refer to ourselves as 'old' not 'Vintage'.

Let's do a check-up – just like we would if you were in fact a vintage car.

How's the duco? Is it well polished and maintained? There are a plethora of cosmetics out there to help smooth out the wrinkles and 'bingles' for both females and males. Skin is a living organism and needs feeding from both outside and inside.

How are the tyres, nice and bouncy or a bit worn and flat? See a Podiatrist on a regular basis. Get the bunions fixed and support the flat arches. Killer heels might be out but there are plenty of smart, sexy shoes out there that don't come from Paul Carrols. Men you don't have to settle for Velcro fastenings unless it's for round the house, a well shod foot is an attractive one.

Let's look at the upholstery. Is it a bit worn and saggy in places? Tone up those muscles with exercise, especially weights and strength ones. Even top athletes lose 50% of their muscles after one month of no exercise. Muscles burn up calories or kilojoules since we have gone all continental these days, so more exercise means more muscle and less fat. Though a bit of padding isn't a bad thing on the vintage model, it fills out the wrinkles, like Polyfilla. Where I come from there is an old saying, 'you either widen or you wizen as you get older,' but I am sure there is a happy medium. There's also room for a bit of cheating with the help of some uplifting, contouring and general squeezing in of the surplus, under the outer coverings.

What about rusty joints? Oil and exercise are what they need. Sitting around won't get them moving it will just expand the rear end. Fish oil capsules inside and exercise outside will loosen them up and stop the creaks and groans.

Time to check under the bonnet. Is the engine running smoothly? Have regular check ups with your Medico. Keep the heart pumping and it won't seize up. If the heart is purring along nicely everything else will be good. The radiator and the fluid exchanges will be spot on – circulation is vital for both cars and humans.

How's the steering? A bit jerky and rusty maybe with a tendency to run off the track from time to time. All it needs is more use and a bit of balancing. Things like Tai Chi where you have to stand on one leg are good. After all the Chinese Vintage models all go out into the open spaces every morning and do it and they live to a ripe old age. The brain needs to be on the ball if it is going to steer well. Read and think about what you have read – a Discussion Group or Book Club could help here. Volunteer to do something that's new to you and you not only get brain stimulation but social contact as well. Keep learning new things like another language that really stirs up the brain cells. TAFE does everything from Aslan to Vietnamese and then you can book a holiday to the country whose language you have learnt so you can practice on the natives. TAFE also teaches a myriad of other courses and with time on your hands you can learn something you have always wanted to try. What if your paintings don't end up in the National Gallery – there's always the 'loo' and at least it will be a talking point. Learn about computers and then write your life story for your family. After all once you have gone, who will know all the family history, it will be gone for ever. Unfortunately we don't seem to get interested in it until we hit mid-life and often by then it's too late to get the information.

Now we need to look at fuel. You wouldn't put rubbish petrol and oil in your Vintage car so why would you put it in the vehicle that is your body. The best maxim is 'keep it simple'. Lots of fresh vegies and fruit with a bit of good quality protein daily and eat everything as near to nature as possible. Use whole grains and avoid white flour and white sugar like the plague. All processed foods are only that way because they have had a lot of chemicals added to process them or preserve them – shelf life is the mantra, not good health for the customer. This doesn't mean you can't indulge occasionally, because if you eat and drink well most of the time your Vintage body will forgive you and cope with the odd fall from grace.

Problems with the exhaust pipe? Have a check up with your Naturopath. Perhaps your bowel flora aren't in balance and that's easy to fix through diet and supplements.

Spluttering a bit going up hills? Again it could be a simple adjustment to the carburettor by fixing what is missing in the energy department. It might be iron or possibly a thyroid problem and a quick blood test will soon sort that out.

So here you are, looking trim, bursting with energy but still sitting in the garage! Open those doors, turn on the ignition, let go of the hand brake and get out there and rally with all those other Vintage people. There's plenty of life in the old car yet. After all you are 'Vintage' not 'Vinished!'

The Retired Men

You see them in Woolies and also in Coles
and I'm sure they're in Aldi in the same roles.
They come in all sizes placid or wired
but one thing in common, they are all retired
There's the 'Sergeant Major,' he's got a list
whilst she pushes the trolley, the decisions are his.
He'll check all the prices, the cheaper the better
she packs the trolley and it must be to the letter.
Then there's the opposite, the meek and the mild
he pushes the trolley and acts like a child.
Whilst she makes the decisions, no reference to him
she wears the trousers and always looks grim.
But perhaps the most pitiful are discarded outside
to sit on a bench, whilst she's occupied.
They sit there in silence, glazed look in the eye
not sure of their place as the world passes by.
They don't talk to each other in case they confess
that since they've retired, their life is a mess.
They could have been labourers, bankers or others
but once they've retired, they all feel like brothers.
Their wives are all busy, their life hasn't changed
still the same routine that keeps them engaged.
The family, the housework, the coffees and cake
so it's only the shopping where he can partake.
But thank God for the Men's Shed where it's only the boys
it keeps them all happy, as they play with their toys.

What Comes Around Goes Around

Blake Withers bent down and pulled the key to his Grandmother's house out of the cat door. This was not a social visit as it was Tuesday and he knew she would be at Bingo all day. He unlocked the door, put the key back where he had found it and walked into the house.

Everything was very clean, neat and orderly, like his Gran. Everything was in its place and he knew exactly where the money would be because he had overheard a conversation between his Mother and his Gran one day.

"Now Debbie," his Gran had said, "after I am dead look in the linen cupboard. There's a loose floorboard under your Dad's old tool chest and there is a stash of money underneath it I've saved. Don't tell anyone else because I want you to have it. Your brother has had his share over the years and a lot of good it's done him, I don't think."

Neither of the two women had realized he was even in the house at the time so he had slipped quietly away with the priceless information.

Now he needed the money and badly. His drug habit had got out of control and he had promised his supplier that he would pay off what he owed today after he got paid for a job he had done. But that hadn't happened because he hadn't turned up to finish the job for a couple of days when he was 'off his face' and what he got barely paid his bus fare home.

It wouldn't be so bad but his supplier was Big Jock,

a man who didn't mince words – just faces. Unless he was in a really benevolent mood when he would let one of his 'minders' do it for him.

Blake, who was very undersized and weedy because he hardly ate these days, was no match for any of them.

By now he had reached the linen cupboard and opening the door pulled out the tool chest onto the hallway carpet. He felt around and couldn't find the loose board at first but then one moved slightly under his hand and he was able to pull it up. He cursed himself for not bringing a torch but put his hand into the hole. It was quite deep and smelt earthy but his finger touched plastic, and he hauled a black garbage bag to the surface.

With trembling fingers he pulled it open and there were bundles of $50 notes. He counted one and it was $500 so as there were ten, even his poor maths could work out there must be $5000. This would pay off his debt and leave some over to buy more. Suddenly the day got brighter.

Carefully he replaced the floorboard and the toolbox and closed the door of the linen cupboard. He checked there were no marks on the carpet and everything looked normal, then, carrying his booty he left the house, after first checking there were no nosy neighbours around, before he walked down the driveway.

A bus that would take him into town came just as he reached the bus stop and a couple of minutes later he was well away from the scene of his crime.

Tommy Jones of no fixed address, well known vagrant in the local Magistrate's Court and not to be trifled with when drunk, stood in the doorway opposite the TAB. He could see his mates George and Fred standing outside sucking on their 'rollies' whilst they waited for the next race to start. He couldn't join them though as his last appearance in the Court had been for being drunk and disorderly when he had trashed part of the TAB, so he was now banned from going within fifty metres of it.

It was a cold day and he shivered in his thin overcoat and thought longingly of a hot meal and a cup of coffee in the local café – but he hadn't any money and it was a week to next pension day.

He didn't take a lot of notice of the weedy young guy who got off the bus at the nearby stop until he put down the black garbage bag he was carrying to light a cigarette. Then to Tommy's surprise, he walked away leaving the garbage bag behind.

Tommy had lived on the streets for many years between stints in jail and he had very quick reflexes, so by the time the young lad realized and came back, the garbage bag was under Tommy's overcoat and he had disappeared down a nearby alley.

The young man rushed up and down frantically and then crossed over the road to George and Fred.

"Did you see anyone pick up a garbage bag over the road just now?" he asked.

George and Fred, who had seen everything, shook their heads.

"No mate," said Fred, "didn't see a thing. Something important was it?"

"A lot of money," blurted out Blake in his panic. "I've got to find it."

"How'd you get here?" asked George in a friendly manner.

"By bus," replied Blake.

"Ah! You probably left it on the bus then son. Get on to Lost Property they'll put you right."

Blake searched up and down again for a while then with shoulders drooping he slouched off up the street.

Fred and George waited until he was out of sight and then rushed across the road and down the alley and into the local café. Tommy was sitting at a table with a cup of coffee and a big plate of eggs, sausages, tomatoes and beans in front of him. The garbage bag was on the chair beside him.

The two men sat down at the table and after a few general comments about the weather Fred said,

"What's in the bag Tommy?"

"Just rubbish. I'll put it in the bin when I go out of here."

"Pity you can't come into the TAB," said George. "We've got a cert for the 11 o'clock at Richmond today. Mate of mine knows the trainer," and here he tapped the side of his nose, "might be a little bit of extra oomph in the nag, if you know what I mean."

"Well I can't go into the TAB you know that. Besides I ain't got no money."

"That's a real shame," said Fred. "50-1 they're offering. George and me have both put our shirts on it already before the odds come down."

Tommy shifted in his seat. He hadn't counted the money and had pulled out a $50 note to pay for his meal but he knew there were plenty more where that came from and at 50-1 there could be a lot more. The old gambling instinct was strong but he wasn't sure how much he could trust his mates.

"Well gotta go," said Fred. "Race starts in five minutes but we'll let you know how much we win."

The two men got up from the table and it was too much for Tommy. He thrust the garbage bag towards them.

"Put this on that cert for me," he gasped, "and I'll wait here for my winnings."

George and Fred could barely contain their grins as they left the café and once outside looked in the bag and counted the money.

"Nearly 5,000 bucks," said George. "not a bad day at the TAB eh Fred?"

They were still chortling as they emerged from the alley just as a black Mercedes with tinted windows rolled slowly past. A very white faced Blake was peering out of the back window and sitting next to a man who could have been a stand in for the Incredible Hulk.

"There it is," he shouted, "those two blokes had it all the time."

The car stopped. The passenger window in the front rolled slowly down and Big Jock's face appeared.

"Well, well," he said, "if it isn't George and Fred and carrying a black garbage bag I believe. What would be in it I wonder?"

"Just rubbish," stuttered George in a trembly voice.

"Then let me dispose of it for you," said Big Jock, holding out a hand the size of a dinner plate, each finger embellished with a large spiky gold ring.

George handed it over. Big Jock closed the window and as the car moved slowly down the road, he passed it to the man in the back.

"Count it," he said.

"$4,950 Boss" said the man.

"Good. Just enough to pay off your debt Blake," said Big Jock.

"But I only owe you $3000," said Blake

"I charge a verra large interest rate," said Big Jock.

The car slowed almost to a stop and the man in the back seat opened the door and pushed Blake out onto the road. The car then sped away.

Bruised and battered, Blake eventually arrived home to find his mother sitting at the kitchen table crying.

"What's happened?" he said.

"It's your Gran," sobbed his Mother. "She won the big prize at Bingo and got so excited she had a heart attack and died."

Blake sat down heavily on the old sofa.

"But it's not all bad,' said his Mother cheering up. "She has left you some money hidden in her linen cupboard under that old toolbox that belonged to your Grandad. She gave me some a few months ago to buy the car and said what was left was for you. Let's go round and get it shall we?"

What's In It For Me?

Charlie Thomas was smoking his pipe and leaning on the gate to his cottage enjoying the warmth of the late spring sunshine on his back. His old dog, Fred, was sprawled on the path beside him. His daughter, Kerry, was cleaning the cottage and Charlie always got out of the way on the day she came to clean.

"Mad woman and soap suds," was the way he described it to his cronies at the pub.

Since his wife Sally had died 5 years ago, Kerry had taken on responsibility for him, but she was like a whirlwind, always in a hurry and rushing to get somewhere else. Charlie wished she would let him do his own housework. He was quite capable but once you turned 70 everybody thought you were past it. Now aged 76 he didn't have much to do. His vegetable garden kept him a bit busy and the odd repair job for people in the village, but they were mostly for the older people and they were fast disappearing. The young ones all had electronic gizmos and Charlie didn't understand them at all.

The village was practically deserted during the day and it was just a dormitory now. Most of the farms had been sold off for housing estates and the children were all bussed to school in the nearby town or driven in their parent's SUVs.

His musings were interrupted by a screech of brakes

and a large Estate Wagon pulled up by his gate. Charlie sighed as the ponderous bulk of Muriel Osborne, the Vicar's wife, climbed out. She bore down upon him like a battleship, he thought, with her large prow thrust before her.

"Mr. Thomas," she said, "how are you today? I do hope your rheumatism is not too painful."

Charlie forbore to say he didn't have rheumatism and just replied.

"Morning, Mrs. Osborne."

"I've come about the churchyard grass," said Mrs. Osborne. "It's got very long this year and needs a lot of mowing."

"Yes," said Charlie, "I was thinking about that the other day when I was up there. I'll do it in a day or so when it's dried out a bit more."

"Ah," said Mrs. Osborne, "now are you sure you are up to it. It's quite a big job for you these days and I am sure we could get someone else to take it over. The Vicar and I were only discussing it at breakfast this morning."

She didn't mention that they were discussing it from quite opposing viewpoints.

The Vicar had looked up from his latest gardening catalogue and said,

"I think Charlie should be allowed to make the decision himself. He has done the job for years and will be very hurt if it's taken away from him."

"You are too soft Bertram," replied his wife.

"Perhaps I am my dear, but I believe my job description is to care for the poor, the lame and the hurt. Charlie keeps the job as long as he wants it. Now I am going to restrain Virginia Creeper. She is climbing into Mr. Lincoln's bed again and I must uphold the moral values of the parish."

With that he picked up his secateurs and shambled out into the garden.

"Of course I can do it," said Charlie, "I'll get my scythe sharpened and it will be no bother."

"Well that's another thing," said Mrs. Osborne, "I will bring along the Vicar's Whipper Snipper for you to use. It will be much easier and quicker for you and the job will be done in no time."

"Don't like them," said Charlie, "noisy things and they gets all tangled up in long grass."

"Nonsense, Mr. Thomas. You just need some more practice, now when will you do it?"

"Thursday, if weather permits," said Charlie.

"Splendid! I will meet you at the churchyard at 8am and no more arguing Mr. Thomas I will bring the Whipper Snipper with me. We have to look after you these days you know. Goodbye Mr. Thomas. The Vicar will be sure to thankyou in church on Sunday of course."

And, with that she swept away and Charlie thought to himself that her stern would not disgrace a battleship either.

"Mentioned in despatches at last," he muttered, "but what's in it for me?"

At that moment Kerry came out of the cottage.

"All done for this week Dad," she said. "There's a shepherd's pie in the oven for your dinner and it will be ready in half an hour so don't forget it's there. What did the old trout want?"

"The graveyard grass cutting," replied Charlie.

"Oh really Dad, It's too much for you now. Why didn't you tell her to get someone else? Now I must rush. Bye."

She gave him a quick peck on his whiskery cheek and climbing into her car, drove rapidly away.

Charlie sighed. Women, they were always bossing a man around. Not that Sally had been like that, they had always seen eye to eye.

As she drove away Muriel saw Kerry come out of the cottage and speak to her father. "Lucky he's got Kerry," she thought, "but she can only do so much with three young children to look after. Charlie has gone downhill fast since Sally died like these old men usually do once their wives have gone. Perhaps Kerry will persuade him not to do the grass cutting this year. I hoped I would put him off by mentioning the Whipper Snipper but he is just as stubborn as Bertram. How did I end up in this village as the Vicar's wife?" she pondered. "I know Vicar's daughters tend to marry Vicars but Bertram has no ambition and all he wants to do is potter in his garden and read gardening catalogues. I should have married Howard Strange. He is a Bishop now and I could have put up with the fact he is a bit on the short and fat side and quite ruthless.

Sometimes I wonder which of us is the Vicar. If I didn't take responsibility things would never get done. It's me who has to go to see old Charlie about the churchyard grass, left to Bertram it could cover the church and he wouldn't notice. But he is a wily old bird for all that absentminded nonsense. Like this morning he always has a biblical quote to trot out and undermine my argument. Perhaps it will rain for the rest of the week and the problem will be postponed."

As he lay in bed that night Charlie was also wishing it would rain for the rest of the week. He hated Whipper Snippers and didn't want to use the noisy thing. Then he had an idea.

Thursday morning was bright and sunny and Charlie was at the churchyard before 8am. He carried his newly sharpened scythe and hid it behind the church.

When Mrs. Osborne arrived he was waiting at the gate.

"Good morning, Mr. Thomas," she said, and going round the back of her wagon, she lifted out the Whipper Snipper.

"Here's a can of fuel, which should be enough and some spare cord," she said, "and I brought the tool kit in case you have any problems."

"Thank you," said Charlie, taking all the gear and laying it on the grass.

"Now, I will be back around midday as I have to go into town to a Council Meeting, so I will pick everything up then. Thank you, Mr. Thomas. Goodbye."

Driving away down the lane, Muriel was puzzled by the change in Charlie's attitude. "He didn't seem bothered by the Whipper Snipper after all," she thought. But she still didn't have a good feeling about it and wondered if she should ring her husband and ask him to go round and check up on Charlie later that morning, but then she remembered Bertram never answered the phone and had never mastered the 'Answer Phone' so it would be a waste of time. With a sigh she pulled out onto the Highway and carried on to the Council Chambers for her meeting.

Charlie watched as she drove away and as soon as she was out of sight, he carefully poured half the fuel out onto the ground so it would look as if he had used it. Next he smeared some green grass over the bottom of the Whipper Snipper so it looked stained, then he left it lying on the ground and went and got his scythe.

He loved the rhythm of the sweeping strokes of the scythe and the swish, swish noise it made as the grass fell away either side of the blade. He could hear the birds and a little green grass snake had time to wriggle away to safety as he approached.

As he mowed around the gravestones he noticed the

inscriptions and they brought back memories of the past. Dick Oates and Ted Smith were side by side. They had been his best friends all his life. They had been to school together, played football and cricket when the village had teams, and darts in the pub as they got too old to chase around. He missed their company and felt very lonely all of a sudden.

Rosie Styles, that name brought back memories and a smile to his face. She had been a wild one that Rosie, but pretty as a picture with her black curls and huge brown eyes.

"Gypsy blood there," said the village Gossips. "She'll be no good."

Rosie had proved them right as her twin boys were born a couple of months after she married Frank Styles the blacksmith. Even worse they both had bright red hair and Frank's hair was as black as Rosie's. One of them was lying next to his mother after crashing his motor bike into a tree at 21.

After about an hour and a half he had done about half the job but the sun, which had been pleasantly warm when he started, now felt very hot and he was sweating profusely. He had shed his jacket and pullover and was down to his shirt sleeves but his arms felt very tired and he had dug the point of the scythe into the ground several times.

Time for a rest he thought and went and got his pack from under the shade of a tree. He had finished close by Sally's grave and went and sat down on it leaning against the gravestone.

"I'll have a cup of tea with you Sally," he said.

He poured the tea from his flask but his hands were very shaky and he spilt quite a bit. Then he tried to unwrap his cheese and pickle sandwiches but he was having difficulty as his left arm felt stiff and his hand couldn't grasp the sandwich properly. Suddenly a sharp pain in his chest made him gasp. He couldn't breathe and felt as if he was choking. Maybe this is what was in it for me was his last thought.

A crow on a nearby tree spotted the sandwiches lying on the grass and approached gingerly. The old man lying next to them didn't move but you never knew with humans. He crept closer in that sideways walk crow's use when they aren't sure about something but when there was still no movement, he was suddenly emboldened, and rushed forward grabbed a sandwich quickly and flew up into his tree with his booty.

Muriel was feeling very pleased with herself as she drove home from her meeting and turned into the lane that led up to the church. It had all gone very well. She was a good Chairperson and had managed to keep everyone on track so they finished on time. In fact the church clock was just striking twelve as she stopped by the gate.

She was quite surprised though to see the Whipper Snipper still lying on the grass where she had left it that morning but it looked as if it had been used so maybe Charlie had finished and gone home. Then she looked around and saw there was still a lot of long grass inside the churchyard.

Perhaps it was too much for him after all she thought and started to load things back into her wagon. But she felt uneasy and decided she had better see how much he had done, so she pushed open the gate and went across the churchyard to where she could see the grass was cut. As she made her way there she could also see a lot of crows on the ground who flew away as she approached. Then she saw something else lying on the ground by one of the gravestones.

"Oh my God!" she said. "It's Charlie.....Charlie, Charlie, are you alright?"

Even as she said it and bent down by the old man she could see he wasn't alright – he was dead.

It was far too late for CPR so she pulled out her mobile phone and dialled the local surgery hoping Fred Clarke the G.P. would still be there.

"Thank God the crows only got as far as the sandwiches," she said, as she waited for her call to be answered. Let's see if Bertram can find a biblical quote for this one.

Don't Get Mad - Get Even

"Pensioner mugged near her home" screamed the headline in the Daily Times as Olive Mason picked up the newspaper from her driveway. She opened the paper and found herself looking at a photo of one of her friends.

"Oh my God!" she said "It's Meryl"

Hurrying into her house she picked up the phone and dialled a number.

"Hi Dave" she said. "Have you seen the paper this morning? Meryl has been attacked and is in hospital. Are you free to come with me this afternoon and visit her?"

"Poor old Meryl" said Dave. "I was only talking to her yesterday morning. Yes of course I'll come with you and I'll pick you up if you like. How about telling Jane and Fred as well? I can tell Jane since she lives next door if you could call Fred."

"Good idea Dave. Meanwhile I will try and contact her daughter Clare and get some details. I don't suppose the hospital will tell me anything as I am not family. Could you pick me up about 2 if that suits everybody else?"

Just after 2 o clock that afternoon a black Honda left the Nirvana Retirement Village with the four friends on board.

"I spoke to Clare," said Olive." Meryl is in room 37 of the Peter Sutcliffe Wing. Apparently she has some facial bruising and a broken arm and she is very shaken of course."

"Do you know what happened?" asked Jane.

"Clare was pretty upset so I didn't like to ask too many questions," replied Olive. "I expect Meryl will tell us all about it when we get there."

"Animals!" said Fred. "Picking on a frail old lady – they should be horsewhipped."

"Personally I would take them out and shoot them, or at least castrate them so they can't breed any more like themselves." said Jane. "Why do we keep people like that in society anyway?"

"Seems to me the police are hogtied," said Fred from the back seat. "My nephew is in the Police Force or Police Service we have to call it these days and he says that even when they are convicted they are back out of prison before the victim's bruises have faded."

"Well someone should do something about it," said Olive, "or it will get to the point that we daren't go out of our houses."

By now they had arrived at the hospital and went in search of room 37. Meryl was propped up in bed with a mound of pillows and they all gasped when they saw her. The right side of her face was just one big bruise and the eye on that side was swollen and closed. Her right arm was in plaster and there was an IV drip going into her left arm and although she had never been a big person, now she looked almost tiny and frail.

"My God Meryl!" said Jane. "What happened?"

Meryl gazed at them from her one good eye.

"Thanks for coming," she said indistinctly as her mouth was swollen on the right side too.

"There were two of them on a scooter thing. I had just drawn some money from the ATM at the little shopping centre near the Village and they slowed down beside me and the passenger grabbed my bag from over my shoulder. Somehow it caught in my jacket and I couldn't let it go so he punched me a couple of times in the face. Then when it still didn't come loose they accelerated and dragged me along the pavement. At that point the strap broke and they took off with the bag."

"Didn't anyone help you?" said Fred in a shocked voice.

"It was all so quick," replied Meryl. There weren't many people about because it was around 2 o' clock. The lunch hour crowds had gone and the school children hadn't come out yet. I usually go then because the shops are quieter. A couple of people came out of the shop on the corner, they called an ambulance and I ended up here." Her eyes filled with tears and Olive put an arm around her shoulders

"What about the police?" asked Fred.

"They took a description from someone," said Meryl. "But like I said it was all so quick and no-one got a good look at them. They had those big black helmets on and nobody got their number."

By now she was looking very tired so her visitors

said their goodbyes and promised to come in again the next day.

They were all very quiet on the way home as the full horror sank in. "Come in for a cuppa - or something stronger," said Olive as she was the first to be dropped off. "We all need something I reckon."

When they were all seated around the kitchen table with their drinks, Dave spoke up.

"We have to do something" he said. "It's no use waiting for the police they just don't have the man power any more. Those mongrels need fixing permanently."

"I agree," said Jane. "But what can we do? We are all getting on a bit and none of us are exactly hale and hearty. I suppose I could hit them with my stick but I would probably fall over in the attempt and it wouldn't make much impact on those helmets anyway. Mind you I could aim for more vulnerable parts."

They all laughed at the picture of Jane with her dodgy hip lashing out with her stick.

"Well we have to do something," replied Dave. "It doesn't matter if we get prosecuted as we haven't got much time left anyway and I would rather risk prison than die knowing I had turned a blind eye." Then he laughed as he realised what he had said. "Well I know that I am blind in one eye any way but I just can't turn the other."

Fred, who had been concentrating on stirring his tea, looked up. "We'll have to be subtle," he said. "We can't beat them head on – especially with those big helmets but if we combined our strengths that would be different. They are going to do this again and again. An ATM close to a retirement village full of elderly people is a prime target. They aren't going to be fazed by fear of the police, like we said they don't have the manpower to watch the ATM all the time but that's one thing we do have – time."

"But even we can't watch 24 hours a day" interjected Olive.

"No, I know that," replied Fred. "But this was aimed at a certain time of the day when it's very quiet and not many people around. We could watch around 2 o'clock and maybe in the morning as well. Nine to ten o'clock is usually quiet too."

"We could have a roster for a few days," said Jane enthusiastically. "There's a little coffee shop opposite that ATM so we could use that then we wouldn't have to stand around and draw attention to ourselves. But what are we going to do when we actually see something?"

"I don't think they will try anything for a few days." said Fred. Next time we see Meryl perhaps she will be able to give us some more details. Like which direction they came from and which direction they took the bag."

"In the meantime," said Dave. "Let's all think of some strategies. We might be old but we aren't daft yet. How about we have another think tank tomorrow when we've been to see Meryl again?"

Unfortunately Meryl wasn't much help.

"It was all so quick," she repeated. I didn't really have time to see anything. It was all so unexpected."

"Well at least you are looking a bit brighter today," said Olive. "Are you in a lot of pain?"

"Not really as they are keeping me on painkillers at the moment but I dread coming back to my Unit and being on my own. My daughter wants me to go and live with her for a while anyway. It's something I always said I wouldn't do but this has changed my whole approach to life."

When the four friends were sitting around Olive's kitchen table again Jane said, "I can still hear what Meryl said ringing in my ears about how it has changed her approach to life. We just have to get revenge for her somehow. Has anyone got any more ideas?"

"We need more information," said Dave. This can't be a random thing they must have an M.O. Somehow they knew Meryl had just drawn money out of that machine and that she was a vulnerable old woman. How would they find that out?"

"Someone is keeping watch obviously," said Olive. Then they contact the two louts who are waiting nearby. I think we start by sitting in that café and watching to see what is going on."

"I agree," said Fred. It's Tuesday today so how about we start on Friday? I think that café is closed on Monday and Tuesday anyway and that gives us time to set up our oppo."

"You two have been watching too many cop shows," said Jane. "Oppo and MO, at least we will have the jargon right. Tell you what, I will volunteer to sit in the café on Friday at those times."

But nothing happened on the Friday or the following week although each day someone was on watch. However the following Wednesday it was Olive's turn and she sat at a table in the window with a pot of tea and her book. Then the door opened and a young man came in. He made a beeline for the other window table and sat down. He was dressed all in black and looked quite surly. He was carrying a bulging back pack and as soon as he was seated pulled out a mobile phone and began to tap on it, but Olive noticed that he was really looking across the road where the ATM was.

Around 3 o'clock there was an obvious increase in people around the shopping centre and the ATM. The young man got up abruptly and went out. As he did so he pulled out a crash helmet from his back pack and put it on his head. Almost immediately a scooter came round the opposite corner and the young man walked across the road and climbed on the back of it. It then took off down the road.

Olive couldn't wait to tell the others what she had seen.

"So that's how they do it," she said excitedly. "One waits until a possible victim goes to the ATM and then lets the other one know. Strolls out putting on his helmet, jumps on the back of the bike and they take off."

"Well done Olive!" said Dave. "You were right. Now how are we going to know when there is a victim?"

"That's easy," said Jane. "We set a trap, a decoy and I am going to volunteer for that because I am the most frail of the four of us, especially leaning on my stick."

"Oh I don't know," said Fred. "It could be dangerous Jane and we don't want you ending up in hospital with Meryl."

"I think we should stake out the café for the rest of the week anyway," said Olive. "They might only come on certain days like pension day."

"Then what are we going to do?" said Dave. "I've got a bit of an idea I would like to run past you but we would need to think about it a bit more."

"No time like the present," said Fred. "What's your idea Dave?"

"Well first what do we want to achieve? I mean do we want to kill these guys or just teach them a lesson?"

"I don't want to kill anyone," said Jane, "but I would like them to suffer like poor Meryl has."

"That's what I thought," said Dave. "So this is my idea."

Several days later the plan was almost complete. The two young men hadn't been seen again since the Wednesday although someone had staked out the café every day. The next Thursday was pension day and once again Olive was in the café. The young man appeared almost immediately she sat down and she hastily texted a message to the others who were waiting for her cue.

About 15 minutes later Jane made an appearance from the direction of the Village and approached the ATM. She was making a big show of difficulty walking and limped up to the machine. Instantly the young man got up and rushed for the door but this time Olive was right behind him.

He was concentrating so hard on putting on his crash helmet that he didn't see or hear Dave's car parked just by the café. As he reached the edge of the pavement Dave accelerated forward and at the same moment Olive jabbed a large hat pin into the young man's backside. With a yelp he jumped forward and was hit by Dave's car, rolling underneath it. Dave jammed on his brakes and leapt out doing a good imitation of terrible shock.

Meanwhile the scooter driver had appeared round the corner but when he saw what had happened he accelerated away, closely followed by Fred who had been parked on the ATM side of the road. Police and ambulance arrived and Dave was still in shock mode.

"He just jumped out in front of me," he said. "I couldn't have missed him whatever I had done."

"That's right," said Olive. "I was right behind him and he wasn't looking at all. He just leapt out in front of the gentleman's car. He seemed to be concentrating on pulling a crash helmet out of his back pack. Is he badly hurt?"

"Well fortunately the car wasn't going very fast," said one of the ambulance men. "He's coming round but he will have some serious bruises and possibly a broken bone or two."

"Oh thank goodness!" said Olive, "At least he is still alive."

The policeman had taken a statement from Dave and didn't seem to think he would lose his license especially as another person in the café had seen the whole thing and corroborated Olive's story.

Later that day they were all back in Olive's unit and very excited with their success.

"One down, one to go," chortled Jane. "It feels so good to have done something instead of just sitting around being victims. How did you get on Fred?"

"I followed him to an old house in the Greetham area," replied Fred. "He just pulled into a driveway and bolted into the house. The scooter seems to live in the drive but I think we will have to do a few reccies around there just to make sure. So I suggest Dave and I stake out the place for a few days at various times and see if we can get a picture of his movements."

"Then what will we do?" asked Olive.

"I have an idea for a bit of sabotage," replied Fred. "I wasn't in the army for nothing you know. Going behind enemy lines to wreak havoc was what I was trained to do."

For the next three days Dave and Fred drove past the old house making notes. Sometimes they would park down the street and watch. It was a quiet street, very rundown and most of the houses seemed to be empty, especially the ones on either side of the scooter owner.

"That's to our advantage," Fred remarked. "I think early one morning would be the time to strike. He doesn't emerge until midday and he probably doesn't go to bed until late if he's anything like my grandkids that age, so we should have a window of opportunity then."

The next morning at dawn, Dave and Fred approached the old house. They had parked further down the road but no-one seemed to be stirring.

"Well I hope we don't have to make a run for it," said Dave. "With my knees I'd be a sitting duck."

"You just have to keep watch at the gate," said Fred and he moved carefully up the drive.

He was only gone a few minutes and then he and Dave went back to their car.

"I reckon we come back about eleven then, we don't want to miss the fun," Fred said. "Let's bring the girls. I think they feel a left out on this bit."

At eleven thirty the four of them were sitting in Dave's car where they had a good view of the old house. The scooter was still in the driveway. Time passed but no-one came out of the house. They were just about to give up when the driver appeared and climbed onto the scooter. He started it and headed out of the drive and turned towards Dave's car. But that was as far as he got because the scooter suddenly stopped abruptly and threw him over the handlebars onto the road and then fell on top of him.

When they had stopped laughing Fred jumped out of the car and went to see what had happened to the driver. He was lying on the road groaning and holding his arm which was bent at a funny angle. There was blood on his face from a gravel rash and he looked as if he would have a very bruised leg from where the scooter had fallen on him.

"Are you alright Mate?" said Fred looking suitably concerned. "Like me to call the police and an ambulance?"

"Nah! I'll be right," said the Young Man "If you can just shift the scooter off me and help me up I'll ring a friend and he can fix it. Dunno what happened it was like the brakes just seized up."

"Funny that eh!" said Fred. "Are you sure you don't want an ambulance?"

"Nah! I'll be right just as long as me phone works."

He frantically pushed some buttons with his good hand and then started talking.

Fred pushed the scooter to the side of the road and then walked back to the car. Dave drove back to the Retirement Village and as usual they sat around Olive's kitchen table.

"That was fun," said Jane. "Let's do it again sometime."

"Funny you should say that," said Olive. "There was an old lady in the paper today who got mugged whilst taking her shopping from her car. It's not very far from here................."

The Power Of Words

They can trip off the tongue
Be frustratingly lost
Used to stir up a mob
To everyone's cost

They can come from the head
They can come from the heart
Bring people together
Or thrust them apart

Sometimes they're cross
Sometimes they're calm
They can be short and sweet
Or as long as your arm

They can be deep and meaningful
Or trite and banal
Range from light hearted banter
To a sneer or a snarl

They can ignite your passion
Expose all your fears
Stimulate your mind
Or bore you to tears

They can ruin a life
Bring a country to war
Cause mayhem and strife
Help repress the poor

They can cut to the quick
They can fit like a glove
They can stab through the heart
They can speak of deep love

But were we without them
How would we fare
Limited to gestures
No stories to share.

About The Author

Maggie Taylor has lived in her log cabin in the Perth Hills for 50 years surrounded by trees, birds and kangaroos.

She has practised as a Naturopath and Kinesiologist for over 30 years which has given her a lot of insight into human behaviour.